Lord E.H. of Cherbury, Will H. Dircks

The Autobiography of Edward, Lord Herbert of Cherbury

Lord E.H. of Cherbury, Will H. Dircks

The Autobiography of Edward, Lord Herbert of Cherbury

ISBN/EAN: 9783337118419

Printed in Europe, USA, Canada, Australia, Japan

Cover: Foto ©Raphael Reischuk / pixelio.de

More available books at **www.hansebooks.com**

The Camelot Series

EDITED BY ERNEST RHYS

LORD HERBERT.

THE AUTOBIOGRAPHY OF EDWARD, LORD HERBERT OF CHERBURY: EDITED, WITH AN INTRODUCTION, BY WILL H. DIRCKS.

LONDON

WALTER SCOTT, 24 WARWICK LANE

NEW YORK : THOMAS WHITTAKER

TORONTO : W. J. GAGE & CO.

1888

CONTENTS.

INTRODUCTION.

LORD HERBERT.

" O, he is the courageous captain of compliments. He fights as you sing prick-song, keeps time, distance, and proportion; rests me his minim rest, one, two, and the third in your bosom: the very butcher of a silk button, a duellist, a duellist! A gentleman of the very first house,—of the first and second cause. Ah, the immortal passado!"

THE autobiographical document presented in the following pages comes to us from about the middle of the century before last. It was written by Lord Herbert, of Cherbury in Shropshire, when, as he tells us, he was over sixty. It has upon it, one would say, the mark of a sexagenarian's hand and style,—the inconsequential garrulity, the tendency to ramble from the point, the ingenuous pedantry, that one might expect in the story of an amiable, a somewhat scholarly, though perhaps not too sagacious old story-teller. But he delights in telling the fairy-tale of his youth, in recalling the story of the quaint and picturesque past in which he so often cut a gallant and picturesque figure, in telling of his travels, his escapades, his honours, of the great personages he had encountered when he was not a little of a personage himself; we see the plumed and laced figures appear and pass, the old cities with their by-gone throng, the cavalcade of gentlemen riding through the rich forest-chases, with the castle-turret in the distance glinting over the yellow tree-tops in the sun; we live in a realm of by-gone state and phantasy, in which princes, courtiers, and ladies move onward in gracious array. The story is invested with the old-world literary halo; it has the interest of a book of travel, of a brave record of gallantry, ceremonial, and adventure; it has the import attaching to the statement of a contemporaneous witness of persons and modes of life and manners of the century before last. But the air of ingenuousness and simplicity that pervades it all is deceptive; this apparently artless and fantastic old story-teller is more cunning than he seems. His book is, in fact, a sort of psychological curiosity; behind its composition lay a complexity of motives difficult to decipher and determine. We find, on getting to know the author independently of this memoir, that it by no means contains a perfect revelation of himself and his personality, but that really it is remarkable for its revelation of the vast faculty of reticence, of the art of putting things, of which this Lord Herbert of Cherbury was the master.

He came of a redoubtable Welsh stock. There was a Herbert—*Herbertus Camararius*—who, coming over, no doubt, in the conventional fashion, was a comrade of the Conqueror. Early in the thirteenth century a descendant of his had lordships granted him in Wales; his grandson, Peter Fitz-Reginald, married a Welsh heiress, and for several generations his successors followed this laudable precedent of marrying heiresses, until the territorial position of the family was consolidated in south-east Wales. Lord Herbert himself, though perhaps his private inclination had little to do with the matter, did not deviate from the ancestral policy in this regard; fortune endowed him when still quite a boy[1] with the hand of Mary, his cousin, the daughter and heiress of Sir William Herbert, of St. Julian's, between Caerleon and Newport. A former Sir William Herbert, of Raglan Castle, made Knight Banneret in 1415, had two sons, William,

---

[1] Herbert states his age as then fifteen. Mr. Sidney L. Lee, the authority on Herbert, says it should be seventeen.

created Earl of Pembroke in 1551, and Sir Richard Herbert, of Colebrook, both of whom fell on Hedgecote Field. This Earl of Pembroke, and this Sir Richard of Colebrook, are regarded by Lord Herbert as the founders of his family, his wife being descended from the former, and himself from the latter. Lord Herbert's great-grandfather was steward under Henry VIII. of the Lordships and Marches of North Wales, of East Wales, and of Cardiganshire; he was, as Herbert says, "a great suppressor of rebels, thieves, and outlaws;" the function of suppression, in view of the multiplicity of these gentry, fell successively to Lord Herbert's grandfather and father, both men of note and distinction, and both in their time Deputy Lieutenants of their county. Lord Herbert remembered his father as "black-haired and bearded," as were his ancestors on his father's side, "of a manly or somewhat stern look, but withal very handsome and compact in his limbs, and of great courage." This father, leaving a family of seven sons and three daughters, died when Herbert was twelve. The period traversed by the autobiography, which covers only about two-thirds of his life, extends from Herbert's birth, which is assigned to 1582-3, till 1624; he lived till 1648. The place of his birth was Eyton, in Shropshire, and the day is indicated

by the title of some commemorative verses:—
in diem natalitium, viz., 3 *Mar.* At the age of
twelve he was sent to Oxford ; when about eighteen
or nineteen he removed to London with his mother,
his wife and family; and presented himself at the
court of Elizabeth, then not far from her end. He
was created a Knight of the Bath at the coronation
of James I.; when about twenty-five, leaving his
family behind him, he went to Paris, one of the
first of a series of visits abroad; in 1619 he was
chosen ambassador to France at the instigation of
Villiers, and the autobiography abruptly closes
with the termination of his ambassadorship and
return home in 1624.

In the beginning of his memoir Lord Herbert
professes to have a philosophical motive for its
composition ; it is to be indited for the benefit of
his descendants, for future representatives of the
house of Cherbury, who, inheriting ancestral
peculiarities of good and evil, may be the better
instructed by its perusal how to recognise and
cherish the good and chasten the evil. He
desires, moreover, to review his past actions on
his own behalf, to recall and examine what he
has done of good or ill for his own private
comfort or admonishment. This prelude, though
it has a touch of Polonius, is, besides being

philosophical, pious and praiseworthy, and likely
to inspire a reverent if credulous posterity with
considerable expectancy of profitable discourse to
follow. Recurring after a perusal of the work to
these prefatory words, one would think they were
dictated by some occult sense of humour, a faculty
which is conspicuously absent throughout the book,
or during some fit of cynicism, for whereby the
posterity of Cherbury are to be morally instructed
by an acquaintance with such facts of his career
as he choses thus with so momentous an air to
introduce to them, seems not easy to determine. In
such recitals and such prescriptions of conduct as
he gives, Lord Herbert seems sympathetically
intent upon a posterity of young gentlemen by
no means likely to possess an interest in philosophic treatises, but, rather, a very choleric
company of young men, a rakish, amorous, duelling,
dancing race of be-ribanded gallants, who in the
future would look back upon this gay ancestor and
his dare-devil exploits with natural veneration. Of
the brothers of Lord Herbert, George Herbert, the
Rector of Bemerton and poet of *The Temple,* is the
much better remembered figure ; he was ten years
younger than Lord Herbert. He was a courtier
before he turned saint ; he had many affinities with
his elder brother, the same choleric temper, the same

love of letters, the same propensity to worldliness. After James I. granted him a sinecure, he left his oratorship at Cambridge to the care of another, to Mr. Herbert Thorndike, and, as Isaac Walton says, "enjoyed his genteel humour for clothes and court-like company." No doubt the saintliness of George Herbert was present in his spirit, in a germinal form at least, from his childhood. Had, however, his circumstances been different he might not have become for Isaac Walton "the holy Mr. Herbert," but have turned out in many respects very much like his brother. For a hermit, for a recluse, for one who has not tasted the vanities of the world, it is no great stroke to deny them; but it was something for the courtly Mr. Herbert, the young rhetorician who used to make such a stir when the king came to Cambridge, and who had so many fine friends and accomplishments; with him denial was no easy task, denial of the train-bands of the world, as he calls them, beauty, money, glory, quick wit, and conversation. He could not quite readily believe these were but "false glozing pleasures,"

> Chases in arras, gilded emptiness,
> Shadows well mounted, dreams in a career,
> Embroidered lies,—

and the pathos of his denial comes home to his reader.

As a virtuous young poetaster of sixteen, he quaintly wrote,—

> Cannot Thy love
> Heighten a spirit to sound out thy praise
> As well as any *she?*

and,

> Cannot Thy Dove
> Outstrip *their* Cupid easily in flight?

—referring to the profane poets—when, poor boy, he did not know the struggle that lay before him, how the instinct to be a profane poet would compete within him against the call to become a saintly one. And the mood of rebellion was often strong upon him; in *The Collar* he has given it dramatic expression in a powerful way :—

> I struck the board and cried, " No more ?"
>   I will abroad,
> What, shall I ever sigh and pine?
>   .   .   .   .
> Is the year only lost to me—
>   Have I no bays to crown it,
> No flowers, no garlands gay !

On the death of the King, the Duke of Richmond, and the Marquis of Hamilton, his patrons, his hopes of court preferment were frustrated, and on his return from Kent, where he passed through his period of reclusion and internal struggle, he had effected the renouncement of worldliness and profane pleasures, and was able to estimate them more truly. But Lord Herbert never formed such an estimate, that brave glory puffing by in whistling silk, which his brother learnt so wistfully to contemn, ever in him found an ardent votary. That as the representative of a great family he should betake himself to the pursuits conformable to his age and condition is no great marvel; but, when one comes to know the man better, to know more of the character of his spirit, that he should rehearse at such length the vain exploits detailed in the following pages, however delightful the entertainment they may now afford, without a touch of irony, or a hint of being conscious of their relative vanity and insignificance, constitutes the romance and paradox of the work and of his character. That the author of this compendium of valorous anecdotes, this handbook of the art of sowing wild-oats with discretion, of this repertory of duelling episodes, of this record of preposterous feats of gallantry; that this rash and habitual duellist, another Tybalt in fieriness and distemper, that this *raconteur* of vain accounts of state and ceremonial, and all the delectable feats of flighty and reckless heroism in the pages following, should at the same time be a student, a

As a virtuous young poetaster of sixteen, he quaintly wrote,—

> Cannot Thy love
> Heighten a spirit to sound out thy praise
> As well as any *she?*

and,

> Cannot Thy Dove
> Outstrip *their* Cupid easily in flight?

—referring to the profane poets—when, poor boy, he did not know the struggle that lay before him, how the instinct to be a profane poet would compete within him against the call to become a saintly one. And the mood of rebellion was often strong upon him; in *The Collar* he has given it dramatic expression in a powerful way :—

> I struck the board and cried, " No more ?"
>   I will abroad,
> What, shall I ever sigh and pine?
>
>   .   .   .   .
>
> Is the year only lost to me—
>   Have I no bays to crown it,
> No flowers, no garlands gay !

On the death of the King, the Duke of Richmond, and the Marquis of Hamilton, his patrons, his hopes of court preferment were frustrated, and on his return from Kent, where he passed through his period of reclusion and internal struggle, he had effected the renouncement of worldliness and profane pleasures, and was able to estimate them more truly. But Lord Herbert never formed such an estimate, that brave glory puffing by in whistling silk, which his brother learnt so wistfully to contemn, ever in him found an ardent votary. That as the representative of a great family he should betake himself to the pursuits conformable to his age and condition is no great marvel ; but, when one comes to know the man better, to know more of the character of his spirit, that he should rehearse at such length the vain exploits detailed in the following pages, however delightful the entertainment they may now afford, without a touch of irony, or a hint of being conscious of their relative vanity and insignificance, constitutes the romance and paradox of the work and of his character. That the author of this compendium of valorous anecdotes, this handbook of the art of sowing wild-oats with discretion, of this repertory of duelling episodes, of this record of preposterous feats of gallantry ; that this rash and habitual duellist, another Tybalt in fieriness and distemper, that this *raconteur* of vain accounts of state and ceremonial, and all the delectable feats of flighty and reckless heroism in the pages following, should at the same time be a student, a dialectician, a strenuous and original thinker, one who laid before himself as his proper task nothing less than the institution of a new system of philosophy, and the development of a new theory of religion, one whom Locke did not consider it unworthy to take up his pen to refute, is indeed curious. His philosophic works were read and commented on by Descartes, a man so deliberately negligent of the writings of others, and Herbert was pronounced by him one much above *des esprits ordinaires;* and Gassendi, at that time probably the most distinguished man of learning in France, wrote, in 1634, after reading Lord Herbert's treatise *De Veritate*, " O happy England, to have, after losing Verulam, raised up this new hero ! "

Lord Herbert was only a little over forty when he was recalled from the ambassadorship of France ; he fulfilled subsequently minor public functions, but his political career then virtually terminated. His attitude during the Civil War was by no means a dignified one; as a public personage he fell into absolute disesteem ; he became known to Royalists and Parliamentarians alike as " the black Lord Herbert." When he set to work to write his auto-biography he was perplexed by the turn of national affairs, and by his own position ; he was, moreover, in breaking health. But his native egotism and vanity were still stalwart, and it is probable that an abiding

motive in compiling his memoir was the presentation
of himself in a popular chronicle, more likely to be
read than his heavier treatises, to a posterity which
might be unfavourably biassed, as one who had
been a person of distinction, one who had been en-
trusted with the care of grave affairs of state, who in
the discharge of them had acquired unwonted respect
and honour. And, as he wrote in his will, "Whereas I
have begun a manifest of my action in these late
troubles, and am prevented in the review thereof,
I do hereby leave it to a person whom I shall by
word instruct to finish the same, and to publish
it to the world by my direction;" that furthermore
he desired to explain and set forth in a worthy
light the facts of his later career, to vindicate and
justify the attitude he adopted during the Rebellion,
and to place himself for good and all on that lofty
pedestal which he deemed to deserve. The autobiography was never concluded; Herbert's manifest
of his action during the civil troubles never appeared;
the name of the editor mentioned in the will has
not come down to us; the autobiography remained
unpublished until Horace Walpole printed a hundred
copies in his private press at Strawberry Hill in
1764; thus the posterity which Herbert would have
wished most to influence did not profit by his
magniloquent exposition of himself. Herbert is

B

not quite unveracious, but he makes discreet omissions; he records those facts, he recalls his connection with those persons, the relation of which may redound most to his own exigeant dignity and honour. His sense of domestic *convenances* forbids him to mention that his mother, at the age of forty, was re-married, her second husband, Sir John Danvers, being ten years younger than herself. Notwithstanding the disparity of years, this union brought with it, if we may trust Donne, who has commented on it, no unhappiness. "She had a cheerfulness," says Donne quaintly, "agreeable to his youth, and he had a sober staidness conformable to her more advanced years." Indeed of his mother, who bestowed such care on his early training, of the Lady Magdalen Herbert, to the exquisite beauty of whose spirit and presence both Walton and Donne[1] have borne such eloquent testimony, Herbert is curiously silent. Various instances of neglect, of curious omission, or of plausible perversion, might be cited. Of Donne himself, with whom Herbert had been brought during his adolescence into intimate contact, and for whom, after Donne's death, he inscribed an elegy,[2]

---

[1] See Appendix: *The Lady Magdalen Herbert.*

[2] See *Elegy for Doctor Dunn*, in Mr. Churton Collins's edition of "The Poems of Lord Herbert of Cherbury."—*Chatto*, 1881.

contained in his posthumous volume of verse, he barely makes mention; Ben Jonson, the familiar friend with whom he exchanged verses, figures nowhere; Bacon, too, who owed his political advancement to the same patron as did Herbert, is, like Selden, absent. We hear, though, of the old, generous, horse-loving Duke of Montmorency, and others of high degree; Herbert comments on being invited when at Paris to the receptions of Queen Margaret of Valois, but says nothing of her reputation; while in the *Satyra Secunda* he addressed in 1608 to Ben Jonson he stigmatises her as "that swol'n vicious Queen Margaret, who were a monster even without her sin." When he introduces humble persons, it is generally because of some honourable diposition manifested towards them by himself; thus he introduces Richard Griffiths, his servant, whom, swimming on his horse, he rescued from drowning in the stream of the Usk, when journeying one day towards Montgomery. During his third ex-pedition abroad, in travelling towards Lyons with the Count Scarnafissi, he rode out of his way to reach Burgoine, in order to see a host's daughter there. But then she was a rarity worthy of examination, for he had heard much talk of her extraordinary beauty from Sir John Finnet and Sir Francis Newport. And with that passion for detail, on which M. Ch. de Rémusat lays stress as a peculiar trait of Herbert, he enters into a minute description of her appearance. The author of *De Veritate* bequeathes to posterity, to those future young gallants of the house of Cherbury, a delectable piece of portraiture; of hair, tied with ribbands of pearl-grey or naccarine; of eyes which, though black, seemed to shoot forth a flame of the same colour; and he even does not forget a gown of green Turkey grogram, slashed from the shoulder to the heel. This heroine seems to have made a lively impression on Herbert's fancy; probably the verses he wrote entitled *La Gralletta Gallante or the Sun-burnt Exotique Beauty*, were inspired by this visit to Burgoine.

One of Herbert's sedate prescriptions to posterity is to keep the company of "grave, learned men," rather than follow the example of "young, wild, and rash persons." It transports one into the region of hopeless conjecture to speculate what in his eyes constituted a wild and rash person. Webster was born about the same year as Herbert, Ford, a few years later; the old fire of Elizabethan tragedy, the old "tragedy of blood," was refined and became artistic in their hands. But the thirst for fierce excesses had not expired; these later dramatists gave, in fact, if a less unbridled, a more intense expression to it than did their earlier fellows. Herbert had all the violent headiness of passion of the Elizabethan, but his passion exhausted itself in action, and he did not betake himself to inditing heroics. Before he composed his autobiography, Herbert was an experienced *littérateur*; he was a student of long habit and standing; he had thought and spent years over the elaboration of treatises of speculative philosophy, and when in his later years he sits down to recount how he challenged this man, or his duel with that, the blood by no means flies to his head, but he sets it all down with complacent equanimity. In his relation of such affairs there is an entire absence of braggadocio, which is really a token of their sincerity and truth; at the same time he seems to have no idea of their often signal outrageousness. Herbert delights in posing before posterity as the perfect and accomplished knight, as that model of "melodious gentlemanliness" which the Renascence conceived; but, above all, as the dandified and reckless swordsman. "And indeed, I shall not speak vaingloriously of myself, if I say that no man understood the use of his weapon better than I did, or hath more dextrously prevailed himself thereof on all occasions;" he perfected himself in France in the usage of the foil, and, in fact, plumes himself on being able to fight by the book of arithmetic. His pages constantly glitter with the waving of steel. The multiplicity of occasions he found for the dextrous use of his weapon, and the facility with which he profited by them, are apt to convey a lively idea of the ferocious nature of the social amenities of his period. Studious, hampered with responsibilities beyond his years, tied to his mother and wife's apron-strings as he was, with little knowledge of the world, and spurred by no very definite ambition, we do not hear of his making any breaches of the peace before he bethought himself to go abroad and enjoy a little irresponsible liberty there. Then he seems to have bent himself to earning reputation as a swordsman. The oath administered to the Knights of the Bath was an antiquated piece of formulary even in Herbert's day, containing many points, as he says himself, " not unlike the romances of knight-errantry." But Herbert took it upon himself to observe the oath with an absurd literality, and found the first pretext shortly after his departure from England, when, one evening, accompanying the Duchess of Ventadour with a train of ladies and cavaliers for a stroll in the meadows surrounding the castle of Mello, he challenged one of the gentlemen, who, in the playfulness of the moment, had snatched a knot of ribband from the hair of the daughter of the Duchess, a little girl of ten or eleven, and stuck it in his hatband; the Frenchman, however, declined the duel. Herbert relates the whole anecdote with a sublime seriousness.

This was but the prelude to a series of challenges, of duels, of hare-brained affrays and escapades. At the ball where he was stationed near Queen Margaret of Valois, while awaiting the dancers to come in, a summons of audacious loudness sounded at the door. Presently there appeared a gentleman whose entrance was the signal for a sudden whisper,—*c'est Monsieur Balagni!*—to run round the room, and for a general subdued stir and sensation. The cavalier was but tolerably handsome; though young, his short-cropped hair was half grey; his doublet was merely of sackcloth cut to his shirt; his breeches of plain cloth. The curiosity and envy of the young Englishman, himself, no doubt, as striking and resplendent a figure as any of the throng, moved him to ask why such attention should be bestowed on this nonchalant, ill-clad person; he learnt that Damien de Montluc, Seigneur de Balagni, was one of the gallantest of the world, having killed his eight or nine men in single fight, wherefore he was much cherished by ladies. The incident impressed itself upon Herbert's memory; and when, a short while after, at the siege of Juliers, he encountered again the Seigneur de Balagni, who one day challenged him to a feat of bravado, he was not slow in response. Balagni, with drawn sword, leapt suddenly out of the trenches; Herbert leaping after him, the two rivals, in reckless emulation, made such headlong speed towards the bastion fronting them, that the hail of shot pouring from it fell behind them. The storm of bullets induced Balagni to pause; he proposed to turn; Herbert vowed that without Balagni turned first, he would stay where he was; Balagni sped back; Herbert, leisurely and upright, followed him, without a hurt, home to the trenches. This was a feat worthy the applause of ladies; Herbert has many stories in which he exhibited a similar fantastic impulse to invite and brook peril, to hazard with rash coxcombry his person for his honour.

He returned from the siege of Juliers laden with reputation, and was much sought after by society. It was about this period that the notable quarrel with Sir John Ayres, of which he has left a circumstantial record, took place. It enables us to conceive vividly the enormous chasm which separates the manners of London of the seventeenth century from London of the nineteenth; to measure the appalling degree to which we have cultivated the art of social restraint, to understand comparatively what poltroons of urbanity we have become. In Herbert's time, notwithstanding the severe enactments against the abuse of the sword, the appeal to its peremptory rhetoric had by no means gone out of vogue; the sense of the readiness with which this appeal was made must have been a fine tonic for the nerves, have aided in imparting to life an often recurring vibration of which nowadays we are not apt to appreciate the intensity. The poor poet in Shakespere's time gadding about London might at any time encounter a rival poet, or some satirised notoriety, and have to stand in mortal defence of the muses and his life. Such episodes helped towards that poetic excitation characteristic of the period, which our latter-day verse seeks in vain to recover. The fray of Montague and Capulet Shakespere could draw from actual scenes he witnessed in the streets of London. He was living at the time, and probably heard of Herbert's encounter with Sir John Ayres. Not without significant reason Ayres believed that this brilliant young gallant, fresh from the wars, the talk of court and town, was paying too much attention to his wife. Accompanied by some of his men, he laid in wait for Herbert in the Scotland Yard of old London. Herbert, attacked by Ayres with sword and dagger, in attempting to alight from his horse was thrown down, his foot hanging in the stirrup and his sword broken. Ayres was about to give him the *coup de grâce*, when Herbert, catching him by the leg, threw him down. They both got up; Ayres was then surrounded by his friends and some of the train of the Earl of Suffolk, the father of Lord Howard of Walden, with whom Herbert had but recently tried to provoke a duel. Herbert, running violently against Ayres, managed to put a thrust in his breast with the broken sword. While his men encompassed Herbert, Ayres found his feet again, and closing with Herbert forced his dagger in him from the ribs to the hip; Herbert, notwithstanding, again threw Ayres, and kneeling on the ground and bestriding the body, struck at him again and again. The friends of Ayres drew him away, the greater part of the crowd retired; Herbert remained master of the field, and presently departed in easy triumph to seek surgical aid. This furious scene,— which Herbert describes with his wonted air of tranquil good-breeding, as evidencing nothing unusual but his own intrepidity,—we can picture again;—the many-coloured crowd of retainers, the wounded plunging horse, the dark, pale, handsome young fellow charging at his opponent, blood-stained like himself, the scuffling, the cries, the flash and clash of steel, and, for background, the red-roofed and many-gabled houses of the Jacobean time. An amusing part of the affair is that the then Lords of the Privy Council, desirous of seeing the weapon which had served in the encounter, sent for the fragment of the sword in order to submit it to sympathetic scrutiny.

This incident was another feather in Herbert's cap; he received various visits and messages of condolence, and became more sought after by society than ever.

With the termination of his ambassadorship to the court of Louis XIII., the period traversed by Herbert's manuscript closes. He returned in July 1624; the frivolous Viscount Kensington, sanguine in his belief in obtaining the hand of the youngest sister of Louis XIII. for the Prince of Wales, and thus cementing the alliance which James I. then desired between Louis and himself, was already in Paris. Kensington and the Earl of Holland had been appointed ambassadors extraordinary in May of that year. Herbert's recall was dated the 14th April, and his position in Paris up to July, when he left, can hardly have been consoling to his personal dignity. The great object of James I. in seeking this marriage for the Prince of Wales, shortly afterwards to become Charles I., with the Princess Henrietta Maria, was to secure the mediation of France for his daughter, the Protestant Princess Elizabeth, and her husband, the Elector Palatine of Bohemia, against the threatening Catholic powers of Germany. The Prince of Wales, having lately returned from Spain where he had been frustrated in his design of securing the hand of the Infanta, the moment was little auspicious for opening negotiations of a similar nature with France;

moreover James desired to impose upon France, in arranging the marriage contract, whatever responsibility might be incurred in the intervention on behalf of his Protestant son-in-law without himself actually engaging English arms in the German conflict. The whole idea to Herbert seemed futile; he wrote to James advocating the policy of possessing actual proof of the intention of Louis XIII. to aid in the recovery of the Palatinate before concluding the marriage treaty; but this straightforward action was alien to the taste of James, always a devotee to intrigue and the devious ways of diplomacy. Herbert knew that Louis had then some intention of proffering alliance to the Duke of Bavaria, the worst foe of the Elector. At the same time the threatening predominance of Spain might render it a political necessity for the Catholic Louis to support a Protestant prince. Incited, perhaps through his friendship with the Princess Elizabeth, the wife of the Elector, to a too ardent devotion to her cause, Herbert adopted an aggressive tone in his discussion of the matter in France; he incensed not only James, but the French ministers, and it was at their instigation he was recalled. Herbert had not regarded his ambassadorship as merely an opportunity for fashionable recreation; a scrutiny of his official correspondence has testified not only to his faculty of surveying and estimating social and political forces, but to his admirable diligence. He returned elated with the vision of court preferment; according to a letter of Chamberlain to Carleton, he was trusting to be chosen Vice-Chamberlain. But six months elapsed before he received the barren favour of elevation to the Irish peerage; he was created Lord Castle-Island,—the name of an estate in Kerry inherited by his wife. The publication of his philosophic work *De Veritate*, the approval it obtained from men of such eminence as Grotius and Tilenus, did not tend to inspire him with any scholarly ideal strong enough to obliterate that of the courtier; he craved still to be the great personage in the eyes of the world; philosophic distinction, merely, was not enough. His lavish expenditure had embarrassed him with debt; his abrupt recall, unfollowed, as it was, by any other appointment, or sufficiently distinguishing mark of royal favour,—for the Irish peerage was a trifle, —was terrible to his reputation. Buckingham was his friend; the accession of Charles augured well for his prospects. Yet Buckingham gave him no encouragement; he did not invite Herbert to his expedition to the Isle of Rhé; and his assassination in the year 1628 must have been a bitter blow to Herbert's hope. It was not till a year later that Charles I. accorded him the English peerage which Buckingham had long promised him, and he became Baron Herbert of Cherbury; this was on the 7th May 1629. Soon after the accession of Charles, Herbert had preferred his suit to him in a letter in which he recalled in set terms his services to the State; he laid indignant stress on the absence of adequate recognition after his return from France; no one had ever returned from the ambassadorship without employment of honour; his abrupt repeal "was the most public disgrace that ever minister in my place did suffer." He was appointed to a seat on the Council of War in 1632; this position he occupied again in 1637; and these petty favours were the most he received. His failure to obtain recognition rendered him only the more assiduous in solicitation; he became untiring as a suppliant for royal favour. The sense of public disgrace seems to have rankled in him always; to remove the public slur which he conceived his reputation had suffered haunted him like a mania. Fifteen years after his return from France he was appealing to the secretary, Windebank, for arrears of pay as ambassador, still due to him, and still commenting on how much his reputation was compromised by his not yet being appointed to some honourable place. The wound seems to gall him as much as ever. Failing the opportunity to distinguish himself in any public capacity, he sought recognition by bringing into play his literary qualities ; a vindication was needed of the conduct of Buckingham in the expedition to the Isle of Rhé ; Herbert undertook to write it. The pamphlet, completed in 1630, failed to help him in the direction he expected ; Charles I. ignored it. He was already engaged in his elaborate *History of the Reign of Henry VIII.*, a work which occupied him during many years ; but his theological liberalism deterred him from dealing sincerely with the subject of the Reformation, which theoretically to him was a matter of small moment ; his delineation of the character of Henry VIII. was too philosophically conceived to be very flattering, and it is extraordinary that Herbert should cherish ideas of the personal advancement he desired through the publication of the book. That personal advancement never came ; seek as he did for it by every means in his power ; by means, too, more often than not, fatally derogatory to himself. His remonstrances and appeals were unheeded ; he suffered, like many others of that time, from the careless ingratitude of the court. When the civil war broke out, entertaining, as may be imagined, no warm affection for the King's cause, he sought to play the part of an opportunist ; he wavered between Royalism and Parliamentarianism,

sincere in his attachment to neither, but intent only
in his own interest; and, notwithstanding, regarded
as he was with disfavour and suspicion by both sides
alike, he lost both fortune and honour.   Well may he
have discovered a difficulty in continuing his autobiography, and of inditing the manifest which he
contemplated of his action during the civil troubles.
As far as he arrives in his memoir his career had been
but a parade of triumph at home and abroad; hence-
forward it was destined to undergo a sorry transforma-
tion, not easily to be disguised.

But turning from Herbert as the delightful knight-
errant, of which we have the indestructible picture
by his own hand, from Herbert as the baffled and
ignoble seeker after court preferment, and from
Herbert as the selfish indifferentist wavering
between two parties in a momentous civil struggle,
and intent only on his private welfare, to Herbert as
a philosopher and theologian, we have a new
revelation of the man.   The extravagant knight-
errant disappears; there is no longer the dependant
courtier, the wavering politician; but a spirit
of profound earnestness and independence; a man
who sincerely strives after truth, and truth of the
highest import; one who made it his quest to
pierce to the ultimate mystery of things. We have
the earliest allusion to his first philosophical work, *De*

Veritate;[1] *my book,* as he familiarly calls it, during the period of his ambassadorship. Herbert himself states that it was begun in England, and there framed in all its principal parts. In 1617 he was attacked by ague, and suffered from a prolonged illness. The good days of his sickness he employed in study, and it is probable that between that year and 1619 he outlined his system, and partially filled in the details. It is recorded of Descartes, a man who had been a soldier like Herbert, who like him mixed in the gay world of Paris, and like him also aimed at the establishment of a new philosophical principle, that when his great idea began to impose itself upon him, he fled into seclusion, became lost to his friends; and, unable to endure the contact of his fellows, did not emerge again until he found himself a victor in the intellectual struggle which his spirit had enforced him to undergo. With Herbert it was vastly different; he tells how, when, ill as he was, he shook one Emerson by the beard, when walking one day in Whitehall, because he had spoken impolitely of Sir Robert Thurley. His philosophic abstraction was not such as to make him forget his perverse instincts; and he was able, while immersed both in business and

---

[1] Its full title is *De Veritate, prout distinguitur Revalatione verisimili, possibili, et à falso.* Paris, 1624; London, 1645.

pleasure in France, to divert his thoughts sufficiently to complete his abstruse work. But we get the first real introduction to the book in a charming passage near the last page of the autobiography, where Herbert recounts that while dubious about the publication of his work, being in his chamber in the Faubourg St. Germain, with the casement open, on a fair day in summer, the sun shining clear and no wind stirring, he took his book in his hand and knelt down to invoke some sign from heaven to guide him. He had no sooner spoken than there came a loud yet gentle noise from heaven, from the serene and cloudless sky, which did so comfort and cheer him that he took his prayer for granted;—a scene which, as he describes it, seems, as has been said, to glow upon the page like an old clear picture of early Italy.

Into Herbert's metaphysical and theological opinions it is needless to enter with more detail than will serve to convey an idea of his seriousness and of his quality as a thinker,—philosopher merely *en amateur* as he is disposed to make himself out to be. The comprehensiveness of the system he constructed is significant of the arrogance of his intellectual ambitions; the life-long devotion he gave to the perfecting of it is the assurance of his sincerity. This sincerity may have had a touch of a superciliousness. "It is not," he said, "from a hypocritical or mercenary writer that we are to look for perfect truth ; the interest of such is not to lay aside the mask and think for themselves. A liberal and independent writer alone will do this." But the great ambassador, Sir Edward Herbert, might flatter himself on the disinterestedness to which his condition entitled him. Hallam's comment on the passage quoted is that it denotes either neglect or ignorance on Herbert's part of the history of thought ; Herbert, indeed, had no reason then to plume himself on any remarkable independency, with the examples of Campanella and of Bacon immediately before him. But Herbert must have profited by the study of the works both of his predecessors and of his contemporaries ; one cannot sit down and formulate theories of perception and ontology out of the unaided inner consciousness. The originality of Herbert's ideas is, in fact, evidence of his philosophic research. But he desired to have the credit of notable originality. There is a singular absence of citation throughout his writings ; such is the case even in his volume *De Religione Gentilium,* which must have involved an extensive research of authorities. And, as in his autobiography, so in his philosophic treatises, Bacon remains unmentioned. They must often have met at court ; Buckingham was the patron of both ;

to George Herbert, Lord Herbert's brother, Bacon dedicated his metrical translation of the Psalms; they both attacked scholasticism; they were both hostile to authority in the sciences. The fundamental principle of Herbert's philosophy was one of intuition; the method of Bacon was the method of scientific observation. The two men widely differed in their modes of obtaining that *Weltanschauung* which was the aim of both. Still, Herbert has occasions of accordance with Bacon, and in omitting to acknowledge his contemporary, it is conceivable that he was moved by some spirit of private antipathy.

Beneath all the fantasticality of Herbert's outward behaviour there lay the sober thinker, the dialectical power and power of synthesis to which his philosophic writings bear testimony. As M. de Rémusat says, in whatever age he had lived, he would have concentrated himself on the questions which perennially engage the world's greater spirits. He rises superior to the religious controversies of his time, but there is no doubt that they found in Herbert a close and passionate observer, and that the turn his thoughts took is explained by his interest in the contemporaneous theological controversies, in the struggle of Sacerdotalist and Puritan, both cleaving to the doctrine of eternal punishment, the Sacerdotalist basing the salvation of the remnant on the grace of the church, the Puritan on the pre-determination of God. Herbert's contribution to the controversy is indicative of the power and loftiness of his thought; he constructs and entrenches himself behind an imposing philosophy before he confronts the main issue. He starts with a theory of perception. There is such a thing as truth. Of truth there are four kinds: truth of the object, which relates to the object in itself; truth of appearance, which relates to the object as manifested; truth of conception, which relates to the object as apprehended by the mind; and finally, the truth which of all these is the highest, truth of intellect. In the introduction of the truth of the object as it is in itself there is a premonition of the *ding an sich* of Kant, but it is a point on which, according to his commentators, Herbert is obscure; Gassendi, however, perhaps most intent on its metaphysical portion, contended that the aim of Herbert's work was that the intellect may pierce into the nature of things, knowing them as they are without the fallacies of appearance and sense. Hallam, who quotes Gassendi to this effect, himself infers from remarks of Herbert that the knowledge of the *communes notitiæ*, the eternal and necessary truths which Herbert contends we have, is accepted by him subjectively. M. de Rémusat, who has made Herbert's theories the subject of exhaustive examination, says that Herbert never asserts at all that the truth of appearance responds to the complete truth of the object. There is little wonder that Herbert's metaphysical faculty failed here, but it is significant of the thoroughness of his synthesis that he should endeavour to incorporate so much. This thoroughness is conspicuous in his treatment of the conditions of his third category of truth, that of the object as apprehended,—that it should have determining individuation, certain limits of dimension, and so on. The final truth of intellect depends upon the conformity of the three preceding kinds of truth defined with each other, and further is conditional on certain principles, principles which being common to every sane and perfect mind, command universal assent. With the introduction of these principles, Herbert seems able to dispense with all the paraphernalia of conditions with which he has surrounded himself, and to make appeal to them as final.

The faculties of the mind are four ; these in Herbert's terminology are Internal Sense, External Sense, the Discursive Faculty or reason, and Natural Instinct. The first deals with the phases of the agreeable and disagreeable, good and evil ; it corresponds to conscience ; the second is the faculty which deals with sensation ; reason deals with the knowledge furnished by the internal and external sense; in all three natural instinct is present as the modifying factor. In the establishment of truths obtained by the discursive faculty, which Herbert calls secondary truths, natural instinct provides a safeguard against the vagaries of scholasticism. What Herbert terms natural instinct corresponds with the Aristotelean noetic faculty, with the *intellectus* of scholasticism, with the common sense of philosophy; it is something akin to the Emersonian over-soul, though not quite so picturesque. It is the vicarious instrument of the universal intelligence of God, a part of the divine seeing incorporated in man; God has given to man not only of his image but of his wisdom. The primary truths, the common notices with which this instinct furnishes us, are not products of experience and observation; the mind is not a *tabula rasa* on which they are projected by the external world; but they are evoked in man in presence of the external world. The mind may be likened, not to a blank book, but to a book only opened on the presentation of the object. The various criteria by which primary truths may be discriminated are such as priority, independence, universality; to call them in question would be to strip man of his essential humanity; the conservation the essential in humanity depends upon them.

Herbert has now arrived at a position from which he may advance into the theological arena. He has got to the standpoint of primary truth. What preeminently distinguishes man is not his gift of reason, but his capacity for religion. George Herbert, who probably profited in some degree by his brother's speculations, has expressed this idea in his own way :—

> " Of all the creatures, both on sea and land,
>   Only to man hast thou made known thy ways,
> And put the pen alone into his hand,
>   And made him secretary of Thy praise.

> Man is the world's high-priest ; he doth present,
>   The sacrifice for all ; while they below
> Unto the service mutter an assent,
>   Such as springs use that fall, or winds that blow."

The common notions, the primary truths, the essential propositions of religion which universally command assent are :—That there is one supreme God ; that he ought to be worshipped ; that virtue and piety are the main elements of worship ; that repentance is a duty ; that there are rewards and punishments both in this life and after it. These are the five pillars of deism ; on these Herbert erects his theory of natural religion, independent as it is of revelation as of the controversies of the sects.

Herbert's *De Religione Gentilium* is an elaborate supplement in support of his thesis; he goes far afield to traverse the various heathen beliefs with a view to abstracting from each his five underlying essential propositions; it is an erudite performance, and has a method and coherency strange to understand as coming from the writer of the autobiography. A passage it contains is very much after the manner of Matthew Arnold; speaking of the divines in connection with their belief in eternal salvation and damnation, he says: "I found that their opinion was not grounded on reason, but some peremptory decrees, which nobody did pretend to know, and I could not think they were so privy to the secret counsels of God as to be able to establish anything for certain; wherefore I left them,"—left them, as has been seen, to establish a gospel of his own, and to become known as the father of English Deism. As well as by Descartes and Gassendi, Herbert's *De Veritate*, which ran through several editions, was subjected to criticism by Nathaniel Culverwel, a Fellow of Emanuel College, Cambridge, in his "Discourse of the Light of Nature," in 1652; by Thomas Halyburton; by Baxter; by Dr. Leland, in the first three chapters of his "View of Deistical Writers," in 1754; and by others. But in Locke, who in his great essay calls Herbert "a man of so great parts," is found the most elaborate of the earlier discussions excited by his work. Into any latter-day criticism of Herbert's theories it is needless here to enter.[1]

It is only natural to expect that Herbert, obeying the fashion of gentlemen of his time, should be a versifier. As a poet he has been but obscurely remembered; it is, in fact, curious, that the autobiography, intended by him to be but the partial index of his many achievements, should come to be best remembered and regarded as his special monument. Throughout his life he seems to have been in the habit of composing verses; to many of them are attached dates, and these range from August 1608 to October 1644. In his autobiography he is silent concerning them, and lacking either opportunity or poetic vanity, he himself published no collection of his poems, but some seventeen years after his death they were brought together and given to the world by his brother Henry, in a volume which he dedicated to Herbert's heir and favourite grandson, Edward, the third Lord Herbert of Cherbury. His contribution to our stock of verse is but slender; such as it is, it classifies him among

---

[1] For an exhaustive examination see M. De Rémusat's *Lord Herbert de Cherbury, sa vie et ses œuvres.* Paris, Didier, 1874. Reference may also be made to Ueberweg, Hist. of Phil. II., and Hamilton's edition of Reid. Mr. Lee gives a concise exposition:

the poets of the school termed metaphysical by
Dr. Johnson in his famous essay on Cowley. Lord
Herbert and the Rector of Bemerton fell upon the
days when poetic effort had succeeded the days of
poetic abandonment; his brother, affected as he was
by the contagion of the *concetti* of the time, survives
because of the exquisite natural vision which the
poetic fashion of his period could not divert and
blind, and because of the import of his ever-recur-
ring theme, the struggle of the earthly desire with
the higher spirit. Lord Herbert is not held by
a theme of any such import, though he has ideas
both lofty and noble to poetically convey. The
poetic epoch following the Elizabethan could not
fail, with such a model immediately before it, to
have a distinctive character of its own; the wild,
unmistakable, lyrical note does, in fact, again and
again sound above the strains of courtly or pedantic
mannerism in the songs of the later choir of poets;
whose most distinctive valuable possession perhaps is,
however, that special quality of daintiness and
fineness of touch and feeling which we know so
well in Herrick, in George Herbert; which we find
in Crashaw; in Lord Herbert's friend, who accompanied him as one of his secretaries when ambassador
to France,—Carew. Lord Herbert was a pupil and
disciple of Donne; he has much of Donne's metrical

and verbal ungainliness; we are never sure that when in full lyrical career he will not suddenly collapse; and the visage of his muse is often most grotesquely disformed. After the manner of the metaphysical school, he decomposes his subject and develops strained parallels; like Donne his master, and like Cowley, he is full of what Coleridge calls the "compulsory juxtaposition" of ideas. Of that wherein he is praiseworthy he has found a liberal eulogist in a modern critic, who has recently edited his collected poems.[1] The volume contains the *Satyra* previously alluded to, addressed in 1608 from Paris to Ben Jonson. During this visit abroad he stayed at the Castle of Mello, lent him by the Duke of Montmorency; and it seems to have been a time poetically fruitful for Herbert; the volume contains various stanzas composed there. Merely an occasional recreation as was verse-making with Herbert, his work affords evidence not merely of poetical potentiality but of actual performance, though it would be hard to cite one completely satisfying effort. Notwithstanding the metrical crudities in which he permits himself so often to lapse, every now and again he demonstrates his possession of a fine ear. In his *Ditty in Imitation of*

---

[1] *The Poems of Lord Herbert of Cherbury*, edited by John Churton Collins; Chatto, 1881.

the Spanish, there occurs the following exquisite stanza, which suggests some well-known lines of Herrick :—

> Then think each minute that you lose a day,
>   The longest youth is short,
> The shortest age is long ; Time flies away,
>   And makes us but his sport,
> And that which is not Youth's is Age's prey.

Though the penultimate line is weak, there is a charming lyrical ebb and flow in the following *Madrigal* :—

> Dear, when I did from you remove,
> I left my joy, but not my love ;
>   That never can depart.
> It neither higher can ascend,
>   Nor lower bend.
> Fixt in the centre of my heart,
>   As in his place,
> And lodgèd so, how can it change ?
> Those are earth's properties and base ;
> Each where, as the bodies divine,
>   Heaven's lights to you and me will shine.

Mr. Churton Collins accords to Herbert the triumph of being the discoverer of the varied harmony and sweetness of the stanza which Lord Tennyson has utilised to such perfection. Besides employing it elsewhere, Herbert has suspended upon it a lengthy ode, *Whether Love should continue for Ever.* It will be sufficient to quote a couple of stanzas :—

> So when one wing can make no way
>   Two joinèd can themselves dilate,
>   So can two persons propagate
> When singly either would decay.
>
> So when from hence we shall be gone,
>   And be no more, nor you, nor I,
>   As one another's mystery,
> Each shall be both, yet both be one.

This is not all; in the final passage of a poem entitled *To Her Mind,* the same critic has found in the staccato construction, in the blending of sentiment and logic, a strong resemblance to the work of Mr. Browning. And it cannot be gainsaid that Herbert, though in his verse generally obscure, and often tedious and fantastic, has occasional fine moods to which he has given an expression correspondingly fine.

After the taking of his residence, Montgomery Castle, by the Parliamentarian forces in 1644, Herbert, almost destitute, made his way to London, where he thenceforward lived. Having professed allegiance to the new rulers, a maintenance of twenty pounds a week was assigned to him, and he took up his abode in Queen Street. Here he found solace in literature; in finishing various of his books. Here, on the 20th August 1648, he died; he was buried in the church of St. Giles-in-the-Fields. Herbert was one of the latest children of the Renascence, and the paradox of his career and character, fascinating as their study must always remain, is explained by the era to which he belonged.

WILL H. DIRCKS.

NEWCASTLE-ON-TYNE, 15*th June* 1888.

NOTE.

I beg here to express my most grateful acknowledgments to Mr. Sidney L. Lee, who gave me permission to make use of his text of *The Life of Lord Herbert* (Nimmo, 1886). Of this permission I have freely availed myself, but I am indebted to him as well in the brief notice preceding for the innumerable points of valuable information contained in his elaborate edition of Herbert's autobiography, a work indispensable to every student of the subject of Herbert's character and life.

W. H. D.

If men get name for some one virtue, then
What man art thou, that art so many men,
All-virtuous Herbert! on whose every part
Truth might spend all her voice, fame all her art?
Whether thy learning they would take or wit,
Or valour, or thy judgment seasoning it,
Thy standing upright to thyself, thy ends
Like straight, thy piety to God and friends:
Their latter praise would still the greatest be,
And yet, they all together, less than thee.

—BEN JONSON.

THE AUTOBIOGRAPHY

OF

EDWARD, LORD HERBERT

OF CHERBURY.

———◆———

I DO believe that if all my ancestors had set down
their lives in writing, and left them to posterity,
many documents necessary to be known of those
who both participate of their natural inclinations and
humours, must in all probability run a not much
different course, might have been given for their
instruction; and certainly it will be found much
better for men to guide themselves by such observations as their father, grandfather, and great grandfather might have delivered to them, than by those
vulgar rules and examples, which cannot in all points
so exactly agree unto them. Therefore, whether their
life were private, and contained only precepts necessary to treat with their children, servants, tenants,
kinsmen, and neighbours, or employed abroad in the
university, or study of the law, or in the court, or in
the camp, their heirs might have benefited themselves
more by them than by any else; for which reason I

have thought fit to relate to my posterity those passages of my life, which I conceive may best declare me, and be most useful to them. In the delivery of which, I profess to write with all truth and sincerity, as scorning ever to deceive or speak false to any; and therefore detesting it much more where I am under obligation of speaking to those so near me: and if this be one reason for taking my pen in hand at this time, so as my age is now past threescore, it will be fit to recollect my former actions, and examine what had been done well or ill, to the intent I may both reform that which was amiss, and so make my peace with God, as also comfort myself in those things which, through God's great grace and favour, have been done according to the rules of conscience, virtue, and honour. Before yet I bring myself to this account, it will be necessary to say somewhat concerning my ancestors, as far as the notice of them is come to me in any credible way; of whom yet I cannot say much, since I was but eight years old when my grandfather died, and that my father lived but about four years after; and that for the rest I have lived for the most part from home, it is impossible I should have that entire knowledge of their actions which might inform me sufficiently; I shall only therefore relate the more known and undoubted parts of their lives.

My father was Richard Herbert, Esq., son of Edward Herbert, Esq., and grandchild to Sir Richard Herbert, Knight, who was a younger son to Sir Richard Herbert, of Colebrook, in Monmouthshire, of all whom

I shall say a little. And first of my father, whom I remember to have been black-haired and bearded, as all my ancestors of his side are said to have been, of a manly or somewhat stern look, but withal very handsome and well compact in his limbs, and of a great courage, whereof he gave proof, when he was so barbarously assaulted by many men in the churchyard at Llanerfyl, at what time he would have apprehended a man who denied to appear to justice; for, defending himself against them all, by the help only of one John ap Howell Corbet, he chased his adversaries until a villain, coming behind him, did over the shoulders of others wound him on the head behind with a forest bill until he fell down, though recovering himself again, notwithstanding his skull was cut through to the *pia mater* of the brain, he saw his adversaries fly away, and after walked home to his house at Llyssyn, where, after he was cured, he offered a single combat to the chief of the family, by whose procurement it was thought the mischief was committed; but he disclaiming wholly the action as not done by his consent, which he offered to testify by oath, and the villain himself flying into Ireland, whence he never returned, my father desisted from prosecuting the business any farther in that kind, and attained, notwithstanding the said hurt, that health and strength, that he returned to his former exercises in a country life, and became the father of many children. As for his integrity in his places of deputy-lieutenant of the county, justice of the peace, and *custos rotulorum*, which he, as my grandfather before him, held, it is so memorable to this day, that it was said his enemies appealed to him for justice, which they also found on all occasions.   His learning was not vulgar, as understanding well the Latin tongue, and being well versed in history.

My grandfather was of a various life, beginning first at court, where after he had spent most part of his means, he became a soldier, and made his fortune with his sword at the battle of St. Quentin in France, and other wars, both in the north, and in the rebellions happening in the times of King Edward VI. and Queen Mary, with so good success, that he not only came off still with the better, but got so much money and wealth as enabled him to buy the greatest part of that livelihood which is descended to me ; although yet I hold some lands which his mother the Lady Anne Herbert purchased, as appears by the deeds made to her by that name, which I can shew ; and might have held more, which my grandfather sold under foot at an under value in his youth, and might have been recovered by my father, had my grandfather suffered him.   My grandfather was noted to be a great enemy to the outlaws and thieves of his time, who robbed in great numbers in the mountains in Montgomeryshire, for the suppressing of whom he went often both day and night to the places where they were ; concerning which, though many particulars have been told me, I shall mention one only.   Some outlaws being lodged in an alehouse upon the hills of Llandinam, my grandfather and a few servants coming to apprehend them, the principal outlaw shot an arrow against my grandfather, which stuck in the pummel of his saddle ; whereupon my grandfather coming up to him with his sword in his hand, and taking him prisoner, he shewed him the said arrow, bidding him look what he had done, whereof the outlaw was no farther sensible than to say he was sorry that he left his better bow at home, which he conceived would have carried his shot to his body ; but the outlaw being brought to justice, suffered for it. My grandfather's power was so great in the country, that divers ancestors of the better families now in Montgomeryshire were his servants, and raised by him. He delighted also much in hospitality, as having a very long table twice covered every meal with the best meats that could be gotten, and a very great family. It was an ordinary saying in the country at that time, when they saw any fowl rise, " Fly where thou wilt, thou wilt light at Blackhall," which was a low building, but of great capacity, my grandfather erected in his age ; his father and himself in former times having lived in Montgomery Castle. Notwithstanding yet these expenses at home, he brought up his children well, married his daughters to the better sort of persons near him, and bringing up his younger sons at the university ; from whence his son Matthew went to the Low Country wars, and after some time spent there, came home, and lived in the country at Dolguog, upon a house and fair living, which my grandfather bestowed upon him. His son also, Charles Herbert, after he had passed some time in the Low Countries, likewise returned home, and was after married to an inheritrix, whose eldest son, called Sir Edward Herbert, Knight, is the king's Attorney-General. His son George, who was of New College in Oxford, was very learned, and of a pious life, died in a middle age of a dropsy. Notwithstanding all which occasions of expense, my grandfather purchased much lands without doing anything yet unjustly or hardly, as may be collected by an offer I have publicly made divers times, having given my bailiff in charge to proclaim to the country, that if any lands were gotten by evil means, or so much as hardly, they should be compounded for or restored again; but to this day, never any man yet complained to me in this kind. He died at the age of four-score or thereabouts, and was buried in Montgomery church, without having any monument made for him, which yet for my father is there set up in a fair manner.

My great-grandfather, Sir Richard Herbert, was steward in the time of King Henry the Eighth, of the lordships and marches of North Wales, East Wales, and Cardiganshire, and had power, in a marshal law, to execute offenders; in the using thereof he was so just, that he acquired to himself a singular reputation, as may appear upon the records of that time, kept in the Paper-Chamber at Whitehall, some touch whereof I have made in my History of Henry the Eighth; of him I can say little more than that he likewise was a great suppressor of rebels, thieves, and outlaws, and that he was just and conscionable; for if a false or cruel person had that power committed to his hands, he would have raised a great fortune out of it, whereof he left little, save what his father gave him, unto posterity. He lieth buried likewise in Montgomery; the upper monument of the two placed in the chancel being erected for him.

My great-great-grandfather, Sir Richard Herbert of Colebrook, was that incomparable hero who (in the History of Hall and Grafton as it appears) twice passed through a great army of northern men alone, with his pole-axe in his hand, and returned without any mortal hurt, which is more than is famed of Amadis de Gaul, or the Knight of the Sun.

I shall, besides this relation of Sir Richard Herbert's prowess in the battle at Banbury or Edgecote Hill, being the place where the late battle was fought, deliver some traditions concerning him, which I have received from good hands: one is, that the said Richard Herbert being employed together with his brother William, Earl of Pembroke, to reduce certain rebels in North Wales, Sir Richard Herbert besieged a principal person of them at Harlech Castle, in Merionethshire; the captain of this place had been a soldier in the wars of France, whereupon he said he had kept a castle in France so long, that he made the old women in Wales talk of him; and that he would keep the castle so long that he would make the old women in France talk of him; and indeed as the place was almost impregnable but by famine, Sir Richard Herbert was constrained to take him in by composition, he surrendering himself upon condition that Sir Richard Herbert should do what he could to save his life; which being accepted, Sir Richard brought him to

King Edward IV., desiring his highness to give him a
pardon, since he yielded up a place of importance,
which he might have kept longer upon this hope ; but
the king replying to Sir Richard Herbert, that he had
no power by his commission to pardon any, and therefore might after the representation hereof to his
majesty, safe deliver him up to justice; Sir Richard
Herbert answered he had not yet done the best he
could for him, and therefore most humbly desired his
highness to do one of two things—either to put him
again in the castle where he was, and command some
other to take him out ; or, if his highness would not do
so, to take his life for the said captain's, that being
the last proof he could give that he used his uttermost
endeavour to save the said captain's life.   The king
finding himself urged thus far, gave Sir Richard
Herbert the life of the said captain, but withal he
bestowed no other reward for his service.

The other history is, that Richard Herbert, together
with his brother the Earl of Pembroke, being in
Anglesea apprehending there seven brothers which
had done many mischiefs and murders; in these times
the Earl of Pembroke, thinking it fit to root out so
wicked a progeny, commanded them all to be hanged ;
whereupon the mother of them coming to the Earl of
Pembroke, upon her knees desired him to pardon two
or at leastwise one of her said sons, affirming that the
rest were sufficient to satisfy justice or example, which
request also Sir Richard Herbert seconded ; but the
earl finding them all equally guilty, said he could
make no distinction betwixt them, and therefore

commanded them to be executed together; at which the mother was so aggrieved, that with a pair of woollen beads on her arms (for so the relation goeth), she on her knees cursed him, praying God's mischief might fall to him in the first battle he should make. The earl after this, coming with his brother to Edgecote Field, as is before set down, after he had put his men in order to fight, found his brother, Sir Richard Herbert in the head of his men, leaning upon his pole-axe in a kind of sad or pensive manner; whereupon the earl said, "What! doth thy great body (for he was higher by the head than any one in the army) apprehend any thing, that thou art so melancholy; or art thou weary with marching, that thou dost lean thus upon thy pole-axe?" Sir Richard Herbert replied, that he was neither of both, whereof he should see the proof presently; "only I cannot but apprehend on your part, lest the curse of the woman with the woollen beads fall upon you." This Sir Richard Herbert lieth buried in Abergavenny, in a sumptuous monument for those times, which still remains; whereas his brother, the Earl of Pembroke, being buried in Tintern Abbey, his monument, together with the church, lie now wholly defaced and ruined. This Earl of Pembroke had a younger son, which had a daughter which married the eldest son of the Earl of Worcester, who carried away the fair castle of Raglan, with many thousand pounds yearly, from the heir male of that house, which was the second son of the said Earl of Pembroke, and ancestor of the family of St. Julians, whose daughter and heir I after married, as shall be told in its place. And here it is very remarkable, that the younger sons of the said Earl of Pembroke and Sir R. Herbert left their posterity after them, who in the person of myself and my wife united both houses again; which is the more memorable, that when the said Earl of Pembroke and Sir R. Herbert were taken prisoners in defending the just cause of Edward IV., at the battle abovesaid, the earl never intreated that his own life might be saved, but his brother's, as it appears by the said history. So that joining of both houses together in my posterity, ought to produce a perpetual obligation of friendship and mutual love in them one to another, since by these two brothers, so brave an example thereof was given as seeming not to live or die but for one another.

My mother was Magdalen Newport, daughter of Sir Richard Newport and Margaret his wife, daughter and heir of Sir Thomas Bromley, one of the privy council, and executor of King Henry the Eighth; who, surviving her husband, gave rare testimonies of an incomparable piety to God and love to her children, as being most assiduous and devout in her daily both private and public prayers, and so careful to provide for her posterity, that, though it were in her power to give her estate (which was very great) to whom she would, yet she continued still unmarried, and so provident for them, that, after she had bestowed all her daughters with sufficient portions upon very good neighbouring families, she delivered up her estate and care of housekeeping to her eldest son Francis, when now she had for many years kept hospitality with that plenty and order as exceeded all either of her country or time ; for, besides abundance of provision and good cheer for guests, which her son Sir Francis Newport continued, she used ever after dinner to distribute with her own hands to the poor, who resorted to her in great numbers, alms in money, to every one of them more or less, as she thought they needed it. By these ancestors I am descended of Talbot, Devereux, Gray, Corbet, and many other noble families, as may be seen in their matches, extant in the many fair coats the Newports bear. I could say much more of my ancestors of that side likewise, but that I should exceed my proposed scope : I shall therefore only say somewhat more of my mother, my brothers, and sisters.

And for my mother, after she lived most virtuously and lovingly with her husband for many years, she after his death erected a fair monument for him in Montgomery church ; brought up her children carefully, and put them in good courses for making their fortunes, and briefly was that woman Dr. Donne hath described in his funeral sermon of her printed. The names of her children were, Edward, Richard, William, Charles, George, Henry, Thomas ; her daughters were, Elizabeth, Margaret, Frances ; of all whom I will say a little before I begin a narration of my own life, so I may pursue my intended purpose the more entirely.

My brother Richard, after he had been brought up

in learning, went to the Low Countries, where he continued many years with much reputation, both in the wars and for fighting single duels, which were many, insomuch that between both, he carried, as I have been told, the scars of four-and-twenty wounds upon him to his grave, and lieth buried in Bergen-op-Zoom. My brother William being brought up likewise in learning, went afterwards to the wars in Denmark, where, fighting a single combat, and having his sword broken, he not only defended himself with that piece which remained, but closing with his adversary, threw him down, and so held him until company came in; and then went to the wars in the Low Countries, but lived not long after. My brother Charles was fellow of New College, in Oxford, where he died young, after he had given great hopes of himself every way.

My brother George was so excellent a scholar, that he was made the public orator of the University in Cambridge; some of whose English works are extant, which though they be rare in their kind, yet are far short of expressing those perfections he had in the Greek and Latin tongue, and all divine and human literature; his life was most holy and exemplary, in so much that about Salisbury, where he lived beneficed for many years, he was little less than sainted: he was not exempt from passion and choler, being infirmities to which all our race is subject, but that excepted, without reproach in his actions.

Henry, after he had been brought up in learning as the other brothers were, was sent by his friends into France, where he attained the language of that country in much perfection, after which time he came to court, and was made gentleman of the king's privy chamber, and master of the revels : by which means, as also by a good marriage, he attained to great fortunes, for himself and posterity to enjoy : he also hath given several proofs of his courage in duels, and otherwise, being no less dexterous in the ways of the court, as having gotten much by it.

My brother Thomas was a posthumus, as being born some weeks after his father's death ; he also being brought up a while at school, was sent as a page to Sir Edward Cecil, lord general of his majesty's auxiliary forces to the princes in Germany, and was particularly at the siege of Juliers, A.D. 1610, where he showed such forwardness as no man in that great army before him was more adventurous on all occasions. Being returned from thence, he went to the East Indies under the command of Captain Joseph, who in his way thither, meeting with a great Spanish ship, was unfortunately killed in fight with them, whereupon his men being disheartened, my brother Thomas encouraged them to revenge the loss, and renewed the fight in that manner (as Sir John Smyth, governor of the East India Company, told me at several times) that they forced the Spanish ship to run aground, where the English shot her through and through so often, that she run herself aground, and was left wholly unserviceable. After which time he, with the rest of the fleet, came to Surat, and from thence went with the merchants to the Great Mogul, where after he had stayed about a twelvemonth, he returned with the same fleet back again to England. After this he went in the navy which King James sent to Algiers, under the command of Sir Robert Mansell, where our men being in great want of money and victuals, and many ships scattering themselves to try whether they could obtain a prize, whereby to relieve the whole fleet; it was his hap to meet with a ship, which he took, and in it to the value of eighteen hundred pounds, which it was thought saved the whole fleet from perishing.

He conducted also Count Mansfelt to the Low Countries, in one of the king's ships, which being unfortunately cast away not far from the shore, the count, together with his company, saved themselves in a long-boat or shalop, the benefit whereof my said brother refused to take for the present, as resolving to assist the master of the ship, who endeavoured by all means to clear the ship from the danger; but finding it impossible, he was the last man that saved himself in the long-boat; the master thereof yet refusing to come away, so that he perished together with the ship. After this, he commanded one of the ships that were sent to bring the prince from Spain, where, upon his return, there being a fight between the Low Countrymen and the Dunkirkers, the prince, who thought it was not for his dignity to suffer them to fight in his presence, commanded some of his ships to part them; whereupon my said brother with some other ships got betwixt them on either side, and shot so long, that both parties were glad to desist. After he had brought the prince safely home, he was appointed to go with one of the king's ships to the Narrow Seas. He also fought divers times with great courage and success with divers men in single fight, sometimes hurting and disarming his adversary, and sometimes driving him away. After all these proofs given of himself, he expected some great command; but finding himself, as he thought, undervalued, he retired to a private and melancholy life, being much discontented to find others preferred to him; in which sullen humour having lived many years, he died and was buried in London, in St. Martin's, near Charing-cross; so that of all my brothers none survives but Henry.

Elizabeth, my eldest sister, was married to Sir Henry Jones, of Abermarles, who had by her one son, and two daughters; the latter end of her time was the most sickly and miserable that hath been known in our times, while for the space of about fourteen years she languished and pined away to skin and bones, and at last died in London, and lies buried in a church near Cheapside. Margaret was married to John Vaughan, son and heir to Owen Vaughan of Llwydiarth, by which match some former differences betwixt our house and that were appeased and reconciled: he had by her three daughters and heirs, Dorothy, Magdalen, and Katherine, of which the two latter only survive. The estate of the Vaughans yet went to the heirs male, though not so clearly but that the entail which carried the said lands was questioned. Frances, my youngest sister, was married to Sir John Brown, Knight, in Lincolnshire, who had by her divers children, the eldest son of whom, though young, fought divers duels, in one of which it was his fortune to kill one Lee, of a great family in Lancashire. I could say many things more concerning all these, but it is not my purpose to particularise their lives : I have related only some passages concerning them to the best of my memory, being assured I have not failed much in my relation of them. I shall now come to myself.

I was born at Eyton, in Shropshire (being a house which, together with fair lands, descended upon the Newports by my said grandmother), between the hours of twelve and one of the clock in the morning ; my infancy was very sickly, my head continually purging itself very much by the ears, whereupon also it was so long before I began to speak, that many thought I should be ever dumb. The very furthest thing I remember is, that when I understood what was said by others, I did yet forbear to speak, lest I should utter something that were imperfect or impertinent. When I came to talk, one of the furthest inquiries I made was, how I came into this world ? I told my nurse, keeper, and others, I found myself here indeed, but from what cause or beginning, or by what means, I could not imagine ; but for this, as I was laughed at by nurse and some other women that were then present, so I was wondered at by others, who said, they never heard a child but myself ask that question ; upon which, when I came to riper years, I made this observation, which afterwards a little comforted me, that as I found myself in possession of this life, without knowing any thing of the pangs and throes my mother suffered, when yet doubtless they did not less press and afflict me than her, so I hope my soul shall pass to a better life than this without being sensible of the anguish and pains my body shall feel in death. For as I believe then I shall be transmitted to a more happy estate by God's great grace, I am confident I shall no more know how I came out of this world, than how I came into it; and because since that time I have made verses to this purpose, I have thought fit to insert them here as a place proper for them. The argument is,

VITA.

PRIMA fuit quondam gentiali semine vita
Procurasse suas dotes, ubi plastica virtus
Gestiit, et vegeto molem perfundere succo,
Externamque suo formam cohibere recessu,
Dum conspirantes possint accedere causæ,
Et totum tuto licuit proludere fœtum.

Altero materno tandem succrevit in arvo
Exiles spumans ubi spiritus induit artus,
Exertusque simul miro sensoria textu
Cudit, et hospitium menti non vile paravit,
Quæ cœlo delapsa suas mox inde capessat
Partes, et sortis tanquàm præsaga futuræ
Corrigat ignavum pondus, nec inutile sistat.

Tertia nunc agitur, quâ scena recluditur ingens,
Cernitur et festum cœli, terræque theatrum ;
Congener et species, rerum variataque forma ;

Et circumferri, motu proprioque vagari
Contigit, et leges æternaque fædera mundi
Visere, et assiduo redeuntia sidera cursu.
Unde etiam vitæ causas, nexumque tueri
Fas erat et summum longè præsciscere Numen ;
Dum varios mirè motus contemperet orbis,
Et Pater, et Dominus, Custos, et conditor idem
Audit ubique Deus ; Quid ni modò Quarta sequatur ?
Sordibus excussis cùm mens jam purior instat,
Auctaque doctrinis variis, virtuteque pollens
Intendit vires, magis et sublimia spirat,
Et tacitus cordi stimulus suffigitur imo,
Ut velit heic quisquam sorti superesse caducæ,
Expetiturque status fælicior ambitiosis
Ritibus, et sacris, et cultu religioso,
Et nova successit melioris conscia fati
Spes superis hærens, toto perfusaque cælo,
Et sese sancto demittit Numen amori,
Et data cælestis non fallax tessera vitæ,
Cumque Deo licuit non uno jure pacisci,
Ut mihi seu servo reddatur debita merces,
Filius aut bona adire paterna petam, mihi sponsor
Sit fidei Numen ; mox hanc sin exuo vitam,
Compos jam factus melioris, tum simul uti
Jure meo cupiam liber, meque asserit inde
Ipse Deus (cujus non terris gratia tantùm,
Sed cælis prostat) quid ni modo Quinta sequatur,
Et Sexta, et quicquid tandem spes ipsa requirat ?

DE VITA CÆLESTI CONJECTURA.

Toto lustratus genio mihi gratulor ipsi,
Fati securus, dum nec terroribus ullis

Dejicior, tacitos condo vel corde dolores,
Sed lætus mediis ærumnis transigo vitam,
Invitisque malis (quæ terras undique cingunt)
Ardenti virtute viam super æthera quærens,
Proxima cælestis præcepi præmia vitæ,
Ultima prætento, divino nixus amore,
Quo simul exuperans creperæ ludibria sortis,
Barbara vesani linquo consortia sæcli,
Auras infernas defflans, spiransque supernas,
Dum sanctis memet totum sic implico flammis.
Hisce ut suffultus penetrem lacquearia cæli,
Atque novi latè speculer magnalia mundi,
Et notas animas, proprio jam lumine pulchras
Invisam, superûmque choros, mentesque beatas,
Quêis aveam miscere ignes, ac vincula sacra,
Atque vice alternâ transire in gaudia, cælum
Quæ dederit cunctis, ipsis aut indita nobis,
Vel quæ communi voto sancire licebit.
Ut deus interea cumulans sua præmia, nostrum
Augeat inde decus, proprioque illustret amore,
Nec cæli cælis desint, æternavè vitæ
Sæcula, vel sæclis nova gaudia, qualia totum
Ævum nec minuat, nec terminat infinitum.
His major desit nec gratia Numinis alma,
Quæ miris variata modis hæc gaudia crescant,
Excipiatque statum quemvis fælicior alter ;
Et quae nec sperare datur sint præstita nobis,
Nec, nisi sola capit quæ mens divina, supersint ;
Quæ licet ex seso sint perfectissima longe,
Ex nobis saltem magè condecorata videntur :
Cum segnes animas, cælum quas indit ab ortu,
Exacuat tantum labor ac industria nostra ;
Ac demum poliat doctrina, et moribus illis,

Ut redeant pulchræ, dotem cæloque reportent;
Quum simul arbitriis usi, mala pellimus illa,
Quæ nec vel pepulit cælum, vel pelleretolim,
Ex nobis ita fit jam gloria Numinis ingens,
Auctior in cælos quoque gloria nostra redundat,
Et quæ virtuti sint debita præmia, tandem
Vel Numen solito reddunt fælicius ipsum.
Amplior unde simul redhibetur Gratia nobis,
Ut vel pro voto nostro jam singula cedant.
Nam si libertas chara est, per amæna locorum
Conspicua innumeris cælis discurrere fas est,
Deliciasque loci cujusvis carpere passim.
Altior est animo si contemplatio fixa,
Cuncta adaperta patent nobis jam scrinia cæli,
Arcanasque Dei rationes nôsse juvabit :
Hujus sin repetat quisquam consortia sæcli,
Mox agere in terris, ac procurare licebit
Res heic humanas, et justis legibus uti !
Sin magè cælesti jam delectamur amore,
Solvimur in flammas, quæ se lambuntque foventque
Mutuò, et impliciti sanctis ardoribus, unà
Surgimus amplexi, copulâ junctique tenaci,
Partibus, et toto miscemur ubique vicissim ;
Ardoresque novos accendit Numinis ardor.
Sin laudare Deum lubeat, nos laudat et ipse,
Concinit angelicusque chorus, modulamine suavi
Personat et cælum, prostant et publica nobis
Gaudia, et eduntur passim spectacula læta ;
Fitque theatralis quasi cæli machina tota.
Hanc mundi molem sin vis replicaverit ingens
Numinis, atque novas formas exculpserit inde
Dotibus ornatas aliis, magis atque capaces ;
Nostras mox etiam formas renovare licebit

Et dotes sensusque alios assumere, tandem
Consummata magis quo gaudia nostra resurgant,
Hæc si conjecto mortali corpori fretus
Corpus et exuerim, Quid ni majora recludam ?

And certainly, since in my mother's womb this *plastica*, or formatrix, which formed my eyes, ears, and other senses, did not intend them for that dark and noisome place, but, as being conscious of a better life, made them as fitting organs to apprehend and perceive those things which should occur in this world ; so I believe, since my coming into this world my soul hath formed or produced certain faculties which are almost as useless for this life as the above-named senses were for the mother's womb ; and these faculties are hope, faith, love, and joy, since they never rest or fix upon any transitory or perishing object in this world, as extending themselves to something further than can be here given, and indeed acquiesce only in the perfect, eternal, and infinite. I confess they are of some use here ; yet I appeal to every body whether any worldly felicity did so satisfy their hope here, that they did not wish and hope for something more excellent ; or whether they had ever that faith in their own wisdom, or in the help of man, that they were not constrained to have recourse to some diviner and superior power than they could find on earth, to relieve them in their danger or necessity ; whether ever they could place their love on any earthly beauty, that it did not fade and wither, if not frustrate or deceive them ; or whether ever their joy was so consummate in any thing they delighted in, that they did not want much more than it, or indeed this world can afford, to make them happy. The proper objects of these faculties, therefore, though framed, or at least appearing in this world, is God only, upon whom faith, hope, and love were never placed in vain, or remain long unrequited. But to leave these discourses, and come to my childhood again.

I remember this defluxion at my ears abovementioned continued in that violence, that my friends did not think fit to teach me so much as my alphabet till I was seven years old, at which time my defluxion ceased, and left me free of the disease my ancestors were subject unto, being the epilepsy. My schoolmaster, in the house of my said lady grandmother, then began to teach me the alphabet, and afterwards grammar, and other books commonly read in schools, in which I profited so much, that upon this theme *Audaces fortuna juvat*, I made an oration of a sheet of paper, and fifty or sixty verses in the space of one day.

I remember in that time I was corrected sometimes for going to cuffs with two school-fellows, being both elder than myself, but never for telling a lie or any other fault; my natural disposition and inclination being so contrary to all falsehood, that being demanded whether I had committed any fault whereof I might be justly suspected, I did use ever to confess it freely, and thereupon choosing rather to suffer correction than to stain my mind with telling a lie, which I did judge then, no time could ever deface; and I can affirm to all the world truly, that from my first infancy to this hour I told not willingly any thing that was false, my soul naturally having an antipathy to lying and deceit.

After I had attained the age of nine, during all which time I lived in my said lady grandmother's house at Eyton, my parents thought fit to send me to some place where I might learn the Welsh tongue, as believing it necessary to enable me to treat with those of my friends and tenants who understood no other language; whereupon I was recommended to Mr. Edward Thelwall, of Plas-y-ward, in Denbighshire.

This gentleman I must remember with honour, as having of himself acquired the exact knowledge of Greek, Latin, French, Italian, and Spanish, and all other learning, having for that purpose neither gone beyond seas, nor so much as had the benefit of any universities: besides, he was of that rare temper in governing his choler, that I never saw him angry during the time of my stay there, and have heard so much of him for many years before. When occasion of offence was given him, I have seen him redden in the face, and after remain for a while silent; but when he spake, his words were so calm and gentle, that I found he had digested his choler, though yet I confess I could never attain that perfection, as being subject ever to choler and passion more than I ought, and generally to speak my mind freely, and indeed rather to imitate those who, having fire within doors, choose rather to give it vent than suffer it to burn the

house. I commend yet much more the manner of Mr.
Thelwall; and certainly he that can forbear speaking
for some while, will remit much of his passion; but
as I could not learn much of him in this kind, so I
did as little profit in learning the Welsh or any other
of those languages that worthy gentleman understood,
as having a tertian ague for the most part of nine
months, which was all the time I stayed in his house.

Having recovered my strength again, I was sent,
being about the age of ten, to be taught by one Mr.
Newton, at Didlebury, in Shropshire, where, in the
space of less than two years, I not only recovered all
I had lost in my sickness, but attained to the knowledge of the Greek tongue and logic, in so much that
at twelve years old my parents thought fit to send me
to Oxford, to University College, where I remember
to have disputed at my first coming in logic, and to
have made in Greek the exercises required in that
college, oftener than in Latin. I had not been many
months in the university, but news was brought me
of my father's death, his sickness being a lethargy,
caros, or *coma viligans,* which continued long upon
him; he seemed at last to die without much pain,
though in his senses. Upon opinion given by physicians that his disease was mortal, my mother
thought fit to send for me home, and presently after
my father's death to desire her brother Sir Francis
Newport to hasten to London, to obtain my wardship
for his and her use jointly, which he obtained.
Shortly after, I was sent again to my studies in
Oxford, where I had not been long but that an

overture for a match with the daughter and heir of
Sir William Herbert of St. Julian's was made, the
occasion whereof was this : Sir William Herbert being
heir-male to the old Earl of Pembroke above-
mentioned, by a younger son of his (for the eldest
son had a daughter who carried away those great
possessions the Earl of Worcester now holds in
Monmouthshire, as I said before), having one only
daughter surviving, made a will whereby he estated
all his possessions in Monmouthshire and Ireland upon
his said daughter, upon condition she married one of
the surname of Herbert, otherwise the said lands to
descend to the heirs male of the said Sir William ; and
his daughter to have only a small portion out of the
lands he had in Anglesea and Carnarvonshire : his
lands being thus settled, Sir William died shortly
afterwards.　He was a man much conversant with
books, and especially given to the study of divinity,
insomuch that he wrote an Exposition upon the
Revelations, which is printed ; though some thought
he was so far from finding the sense thereof as he was
from attaining the philosopher's stone, which was
another part of his study : howsoever, he was very
understanding in all other things, he was noted yet to
be of a very high mind ; but I can say little of him,
as having never seen his person, nor otherwise had
much information concerning him.　His daughter and
heir, called Mary, after her father died, continued
unmarried till she was one-and-twenty, none of the
Herberts appearing in all that time, who either in age
or fortune was fit to match her.

About this time I had attained the age of fifteen, and a match at last being proposed, yet, notwithstanding the disparity of years betwixt us, upon the eight-and-twentieth of February, 1598, in the house of Eyton, where the same vicar married my father and mother, christened and married me, I espoused her. Not long after my marriage I went again to Oxford, together with my wife and mother, who took a house and lived for some certain time there: and now, having a due remedy for that lasciviousness to which youth is naturally inclined, I followed my book more closely than ever ; in which course I continued till I attained about the age of eighteen, when my mother took a house in London, between which place and Montgomery Castle I passed my time till I came to the age of one-and-twenty, having in that space divers children, I having none now remaining but Beatrice, Richard, and Edward. During this time of living in the university, or at home, I did, without any master or teacher, attain the knowledge of the French, Italian, and Spanish languages, by the help of some books in Latin or English, translated into those idioms, and the dictionaries of those several languages: I attained also to sing my part at first sight in music, and to play on the lute with very little or at most no teaching. My intention in learning languages being to make myself a citizen of the world as far as it were possible ; and my learning of music was for this end, that I might entertain myself at home, and together refresh my mind after my studies, to which I was exceedingly inclined, and that I might not need the company of young men, in whom I observed in those times much ill example and debauchery.

Being gotten thus far into my age, I shall give some observations concerning ordinary education, even from the first infancy till the departure from the university; as being desirous, together with the narration of my life, to deliver such rules as I conceive may be useful to my posterity.

And first, I find, that in the infancy those diseases are to be remedied which may be hereditary unto them on either side ; so that, if they be subject to the stone or gravel, I do conceive it will be good for the nurse sometimes to drink posset-drinks, in which are boiled such things as are good to expel gravel and stone : the child also himself, when he comes to some age, may use the same posset-drinks of herbs, as *milium solis*, saxifrigia, &c., good for the stone many are reckoned by the physicians, of which also myself could bring a large catalogue, but rather leave it to those who are expert in that art. The same course is to be taken for the gout, for which purpose I do much commend the bathing of children's legs and feet in the water wherein smiths quench their iron, as also water wherein alum hath been infused, or boiled, as also the decoction of juniper-berries, bay-berries, *chamedris, chamœpetis,* which baths also are good for those that are hereditarily subject to the palsy, for these things do much strengthen the sinews ; as also *olium castorii,* and *succoni,* which are not to be used without advice. They that are also subject to the spleen from their ancestors, ought to use those herbs that are splenetics; and those that are troubled with the falling sickness, with cephaliques, of which certainly I should have had need, but for the purging of my ears above-mentioned. Briefly, what disease soever it be that is derived from ancestors of either side, it will be necessary first to give such medicines to the nurse as may make her milk effectual for those purposes; as also afterwards to give unto the child itself such specific remedies as his age and constitution will bear. I could say much more upon this point, as having delighted ever in the knowledge of herbs plants, and gums, and in few words, the history of nature, insomuch that, coming to apothecaries' shops, it was my ordinary manner, when I looked upon the bills filed up, containing the physicians' prescriptions, to tell every man's disease. Howbeit, I shall not presume in these particulars to prescribe to my posterity, though I believe I know the best receipts for almost all diseases, but shall leave them to expert physicians; only I will recommend again to my posterity the curing of hereditary diseases in the very infancy, since otherwise, without much difficulty, they will never be cured.

When children go to school, they should have one to attend them who may take care of their manners as well as the schoolmaster doth of their learning, for among boys all vice is easily learned; and here I could wish it constantly observed, that neither the master should correct him for faults of his manners, nor his governor for manners for the faults in his learning. After the alphabet is taught, I like well the shortest and clearest grammars, and such books into which all the Greek and Latin words are severally contrived, in which kind one Comenus hath given an example : this being done, it would be much better to proceed with Greek authors than with Latin ; for as it is as easy to learn at first the one as the other, it would be much better to give the first impressions into the child's memory of those things which are more rare than usual; therefore I would have them begin at Greek first, and the rather, that there is not that art in the world wherein the Greeks have not excelled and gone before others : so that when you look upon philosophy, astronomy, mathematics, medicine, and briefly, all learning, the Greeks have exceeded all nations. When he shall be ready to go to the university, it will be fit also his governor for manners go along with him, it being the frail nature of youth, as they grow to ripeness in age, to be more capable of doing ill, unless their manners be well guided, and themselves by degrees habituated in virtue, with which if once they acquaint themselves, they will find more pleasure in it than ever they can do in vice; since every body loves virtuous persons, whereas the vicious do scarce love one another. For this purpose, it will be necessary that you keep the company of grave, learned men, who are of good reputation, and hear rather what they say, and follow what they do, than follow the examples of young, wild, and rash persons; and certainly of those two parts which are to be acquired in youth, whereof one is goodness and virtuous manners, the other learning and knowledge, I shall so much prefer the first before the second, as I shall ever think virtue accompanied with ordinary discretion, will make his way better both to happiness in this world and the next, than any puffed knowledge which would cause him to be insolent and vainglorious, or minister, as it were, arms and advantages to him for doing a mischief ; so that it is pity that wicked dispositions should have knowledge to actuate their ill intentions, or courage to maintain them,—that fortitude which should defend all a man's virtues being never well employed to defend his humours, passions, or vices.

I do not approve for elder brothers that course of study which is ordinarily used in the university, which is, if their parents perchance intend they shall stay there four or five years, to employ the said time as if they meant to proceed Masters of Art and Doctors in some science ; for which purpose their tutors commonly spend much time in teaching them the subtilties of logic, which, as it is usually practised, enables them for little more than to be excellent wranglers, which art, though it may be tolerable in a mercenary lawyer, I can by no means commend in a sober and well-governed gentleman.

I approve much those parts of logic which teach men to deduce their proofs from firm and undoubted principles, and show men to distinguish betwixt truth and falsehood, and help them to discover fallacies, sophisms, and that which the schoolmen call vicious argumentations, concerning which I shall not here enter into a long discourse. So much of logic as may

serve for this purpose being acquired, some good sum
of philosophy may be learned, which may teach him
both the ground of the Platonic and Aristotelian
philosophy. After which, it will not be amiss to read
the *Idea Medicinæ Philosophicæ,* written by Sever-
nius Danus, there being many things considerable
concerning the Paracelsian principles written in that
book, which are not to be found in former writers:
it will not be amiss also to read over Franciscus
Patricius, and Telesius, who have examined and con-
troverted the ordinary peripatetic doctrine; all which
may be performed in one year, that term being
enough for philosophy, as I conceive, and six months
for logic; for I am confident a man may have quickly
more than he needs of these two arts.

These being attained, it will be requisite to study
geography with exactness, so much as may teach a
man the situation of all countries in the whole world;
together with which it will be fit to learn something
concerning the governments, manners, religions, either
ancient or new, as also the interests of states and
relations in amity, or strength in which they stand to
their neighbours: it will be necessary also, at the
same time, to learn the use of the celestial globe, the
studies of both globes being complicated and joined
together. I do not conceive yet the knowledge of
judicial astrology so necessary, but only for general
predictions; particular events being neither intended
by nor collected out of the stars.

It will be also fit to learn arithmetic and geometry
in some good measure, but especially arithmetic, it

being most useful for many purposes, and among the rest for keeping accounts, whereof here is much use. As for the knowledge of lines, superficies, and bodies, though it be a science of much certainty and demonstration, it is not much useful for a gentleman, unless it be to understand fortifications, the knowledge whereof is worthy of those who intend the wars; though yet he must remember, that whatsoever art doth in way of defence, art likewise, in way of assailing, can destroy. This study hath cost me much labour, but as yet I could never find how any place could be so fortified, but that there were means in certain opposite lines to prevent or subvert all that could be done in that kind.

It will become a gentleman to have some knowledge in medicine, especially the diagnostic part, whereby he may take timely notice of a disease, and by that means timely prevent it; as also the prognostic part, whereby he may judge of the symptoms either increasing or decreasing in the disease, as also concerning the crisis or indication thereof. This art will get a gentleman not only much knowledge, but much credit; since seeing any sick body, he will be able to tell, in all human probability, whether he shall recover, or if he shall die of the disease, to tell what signs shall go before, and what the conclusion will be. It will become him also to know not only the ingredients, but doses of certain cathartic or purging, emetic or vomitive medicines, specific or choleric, melancholic, or phlegmatic constitutions, phlebotomy being only necessary for those who abound in blood. Besides, I would have a gentleman know how to make these medicines himself, and afterwards prepare them with his own hands; it being the manner of apothecaries so frequently to put in the succedanea, that no man is sure to find with them medicines made with the true drugs which ought to enter into the composition when it is exotic or rare; or when they are extant in the shop, no man can be assured that the said drugs are not rotten, or that they have not lost their natural force and virtue. I have studied this art very much also, and have, in cases of extremity, ministered physic with that success which is strange, whereof I shall give two or three examples. Richard Griffiths, of Sutton, my servant, being sick of a malignant pestilent fever, and tried in vain all our country physicians could do, and his water at last stinking so grievously, which physicians note to be a sign of extension of natural heat, and consequently of present death, I was entreated to see him, when as yet he had neither eaten, drank, slept, or known anybody for the space of six or seven days; whereupon, demanding whether the physicians had given him over, and it being answered unto me that they had, I said it would not be amiss to give him the quantity of an hazle-nut of a certain rare receipt which I had, assuring, that if anything in the world could recover him, that would; of which I was so confident, that I would come the next day at four of the clock in the afternoon unto him, and at that time I doubted not but they should find signs of amendment, provided they should put the doses I gave them, being about the bigness of a nut, down his throat; which being done with much difficulty, I came the morrow after at the hour appointed, when, to the wonder of his family, he knew me, and asked for some broth, and not long after recovered.

My cousin Athelston Owen, also of Rhiew Saeson, having an hydrocephale also in that extremity, that his eyes began to start out of his head, and his tongue to come out of his mouth, and his whole head finally exceeding its natural proportion, insomuch that his physicians likewise left him, I prescribed to him the decoction of two diuretic roots, which after he had drank four or five days, he urined in that abundance that his head by degrees returned to its ancient figure, and all other signs of health appeared; whereupon also he wrote a letter to me, that he was so suddenly and perfectly restored to his former health, that it seemed more like a miracle than a cure; for those are the very words in the letter he sent me.

I cured a great lady in London of an issue of blood, when all the physicians had given her over, with so easy a medicine, that the lady herself was astonished to find the effects thereof. I could give more examples in this kind, but these shall suffice; I will for the rest deliver a rule I conceive for finding out the bests receipts not only for curing all inward but outward hurts, such as are ulcers, tumours, contusions, wounds, and the like: you must look upon all pharmacopæias or antidotaries of several countries; of which sort I have in my library the *Pharmacopœia Londinensis, Parisiensis, Amstelredamensis,* that of

Quercetanus,[1] Bauderonus, Renadeus, Valerius Scordus, *Pharmacopœia Coloniensis*, Augustana, Venetiana, Vononiensis, Florentina, Romana, Messanensis; in some of which are told not only what the receipts there set down are good for, but the doses of them. The rule I here give is, that what all the said dipensatorsies, antidotaries, or pharmacopæias prescribe as effectual for overcoming a disease, is certainly good ; for as they are set forth by authority of the physicians of these several countries, what they all ordain must necessarily be effectual: but they who will follow my advice, shall find in that little short antidotary called Amstelredamensis, not long since put forth, almost all that is necessary to be known for curing of diseases, wounds, etc. There is a book called *Aurora Medicorum*, very fit to be read in this kind. Among writers of physic, I do especially commend, after Hippocrates and Galen, Fernelius,[2] Lud. Mercatus, and Dan. Sennertus, and Heurnius. I could name many more but I conceive these may suffice. As for the chemic or spagyric medicines, I cannot commend them

---

[1] Josephus Quercetanus published a Pharmacopœia Dogmaticorum Restituta, 1607, 4to. Paris. Bricius Bauderonus, Pharmacopœia et Praxis Medica, 1620, Paris. Johannes Renodæus, Dispensatorium Medicum et Antidotarium, 1609, 4to. Paris. Valerius Cordus, Dispensatorium, Antw. 1568.

[2] Johannes Fernelius (Physician to Henry II. of France) published Opera Medicinalia, et Universa Medicina, 1564, 4to. et 1577, fol. Lud. Mercatus (physician to Philip II. and III. of Spain) was author of Opera Medica et Chirurgica, fol. Francof. 1620. Daniel Sennertus published Institutiones Medicinæ, 1620 ; and Johannes Heurnius a work of the same title, 1597. Lugduni.

to the use of my posterity, there being neither emetic, cathartic, diaphoretic, diuretic medicines extant among them, which are not much more happily and safely performed by vegetables; but hereof enough, since I pretend no further than to give some few directions to my posterity.

In the meanwhile I conceive it is a fine study, and worthy a gentleman, to be a good botanic, that so he may know the nature of all herbs and plants, being our fellow-creatures, and made for the use of man; for which purpose it will be fit for him to cull out of some good herbal all the icones together, with the descriptions of them, and to lay by themselves all such as grow in England; and afterwards to select again such as usually grow by the highway-side, in meadows, by rivers, or in marshes, or in corn-fields, or in dry and mountainous places, or on rocks, walls, or in shady places, such as grow by the sea-side; for this being done, and the said icones being ordinarily carried by themselves, or by their servants, one may presently find out every herb he meets withal, especially if the said flowers be truly coloured. Afterwards it will not be amiss to distinguish by themselves such herbs as are in gardens and are exotics, and are transplanted hither.

As for those plants which will not endure our clime, though the knowledge of them be worthy of a gentleman, and the virtues of them be fit to be learned, especially if they be brought over to a druggist as medicinal, yet the icones of them are not so pertinent to be known as the former, unless it be where there is less danger of adulterating the said medicaments; in which case it is good to have recourse to not only the botanics, but also to Gesnar's Dispensatory, and to *Aurora Medicorum* above-mentioned, being books which make a man distinguish betwixt good and bad drugs. And thus much of medicine may not only be useful but delectable to a gentleman, since which way soever he passeth, he may find something to entertain him. I must no less commend the study of anatomy, which whosoever considers, I believe will never be an atheist; the frame of a man's body and coherence of his parts being so strange and paradoxal, that I hold it to be the greatest miracle of nature; though when all is done, I do not find she hath made it so much as proof against one disease, lest it should be thought to have made it no less than a prison to the soul.

Having thus passed over all human literature, it will be fit to say something of moral virtues and theological learning. As for the first, since the Christians and the heathens are in a manner agreed concerning the definitions of virtues, it would not be inconvenient to begin with those definitions which Aristotle in his Morals hath given, as being confirmed for the most part by the Platonics, Stoics, and other philosophers, and in general by the Christian Church, as well as all nations in the world whatsoever; they being doctrines imprinted in the soul in its first original, and containing the principal and first notices by which man may attain his happiness here or hereafter; there being no man that is given to vice

that doth not find much opposition both in his own
conscience, and in the religion and law is taught
elsewhere; and this I dare say, that a virtuous
man may not only go securely through all the
religions, but all the laws in the world, and
whatsoever obstructions he meets, obtain both an
inward peace and outward welcome among all with
whom he shall negociate or converse: this virtue,
therefore, I shall recommend to my posterity as the
greatest perfection he can attain unto in this life,
and the pledge of eternal happiness hereafter; there
being none that can justly hope of an union with the
supreme God, that doth not come as near to him in
this life in virtue and goodness as he can; so that if
human frailty do interrupt this union by committing
faults that make him incapable of his everlasting
happiness, it will be fit, by a serious repentance, to
expiate and emaculate those faults, and for the rest
trust to the mercy of God, his Creator, Redeemer, and
Preserver, who being our Father, and knowing well
in what a weak condition through infirmities we are,
will, I doubt not, commiserate those transgressions
we commit, when they are done without desire to
offend his Divine Majesty, and together rectify our
understanding through his grace: since we commonly
sin through no other cause, but that we mistook a
true good for that which was only apparent, and so
were deceived, by making an undue election in the
objects proposed to us; wherein, though it will be
fit for every man to confess that he hath offended
an infinite Majesty and Power, yet, as upon better

consideration he finds he did not mean infinitely to offend, there will be just reason to believe that God will not inflict an infinite punishment upon him if he be truly penitent, so that his justice may be satisfied, if not with man's repentance, yet at least with some temporal punishment here or hereafter, such as may be proportionable to the offence; though I cannot deny but when man would infinitely offend God in a despiteful and contemptuous way, it will be just that he suffer an infinite punishment: but as I hope none are so wicked as to sin purposedly and with an high hand against the eternal Majesty of God, so when they shall commit any sins out of frailty, I shall believe either that unless they be finally impenitent, and (as they say) sold ingeniously over to sin, God's mercy will accept of their endeavours to return into a right way, and so make their peace with him by all those good means that are possible.

Having thus recommended the learning of moral philosophy and practice of virtue, as the most necessary knowledge and useful exercise of man's life, I shall observe, that even in the employing of our virtues, discretion is required; for every virtue is not promiscuously to be used, but such only as is proper for the present occasion. Therefore, though a wary and discreet wisdom be most useful where no imminent danger appears, yet, where an enemy draweth his sword against you, you shall have most use of fortitude, prevention being too late, when the danger is so pressing. On the other side, there is no occasion to use your fortitude against wrongs done by women or children, or ignorant persons, that I may say nothing of those that are much your superiors, who are magistrates, etc., since you might by a discreet wisdom have declined the injury, or when it were too late to do so, you may with more equal mind support that which is done, either by authority in the one, or frailty in the other. And certainly to such kind of persons forgiveness will be proper; in which kind I am confident no man of my time hath exceeded me; for though whensoever my honour hath been engaged, no man hath ever been more forward to hazard his life, yet where with my honour I could forgive, I never used revenge, as leaving it always to God, who, the less I punish mine enemies, will inflict so much the more punishment on them; and to this forgiveness of others three considerations have especially invited me.

1. That he that cannot forgive others, breaks the bridge over which he must pass himself, for every man hath need to be forgiven.

2. That when a man wants or comes short of an entire and accomplished virtue, our defects may be supplied this way, since the forgiving of evil deeds in others amounteth to no less than virtue in us; that therefore it may be not unaptly called the paying our debts with another man's money.

3. That it is the most necessary and proper work of every man; for, though when I do not a just thing, or a charitable, or a wise, another man may do it for me, yet no man can forgive my enemy but myself: and these have been the chief motives for

which I have been ever inclined to forgiveness; whereof, though I have rarely found other effect than that my servants, tenants, and neighbours, have thereupon more frequently offended me, yet at least I have had within me an inward peace and comfort thereby, since I can truly say, nothing ever gave my mind more ease than when I had forgiven my enemies, which freed me from many cares and perturbations, which otherwise would have molested me.

And this likewise brings in another rule concerning the use of virtues, which is, that you are not to use justice where mercy is most proper; as, on the other side, a foolish pity is not to be preferred before that which is just and necessary for good example. So likewise liberality is not to be used where parsimony or frugality is more requisite; as, on the other side, it will be but a sordid thing in a gentleman to spare where expending of money would acquire unto him advantage, credit, or honour; and this rule in general ought to be practised, that the virtue requisite to the occasion is ever to be produced, as the most opportune and necessary. That, therefore, wisdom is the soul of all virtues, giving them, as unto her members, life and motion, and so necessary in every action, that whosoever by the benefit of true wisdom makes use of the right virtue on all emergent occasions, I dare say would never be constrained to have recourse to vice, whereby it appears that every virtue is not to be employed indifferently, but that only which is proper for the business in question; among which yet temperance seems so universally requisite, that some part of it at least will be a necessary ingredient in all human actions, since there may be an excess even in religious worship, at those times when other duties are required at our hands. After all, moral virtues are learned and directed to the service and glory of God, as the principal end and use of them.

It would be fit that some time be spent in learning rhetoric or oratory, to the intent that upon all occasions you may express yourself with eloquence and grace; for as it is not enough for a man to have a diamond, unless it is polished and cut out into its due angles, and a foil be set underneath, whereby it may the better transmit and vibrate its native lustre and rays; so it will not be sufficient for a man to have a great understanding in all matters, unless the said understanding be not only polished and clear, but underset and holpen a little with those figures, tropes, and colours which rhetoric affords, where there is use of persuasion. I can by no means yet commend an affected eloquence, there being nothing so pedantical, or indeed that would give more suspicion that the truth is not intended, than to use overmuch the common forms prescribed in schools. It is well said by them, that there are two parts of eloquence necessary and recommendable; one is, to speak hard things plainly, so that when a knotty or intricate business, having no method or coherence in its parts, shall be presented, it will be a singular part of oratory to take those parts asunder, set them together aptly, and so exhibit them to the understanding. And this part of rhetoric I much commend to every body, there being no true use of speech but to make things clear, perspicuous, and manifest, which otherwise would be perplexed, doubtful, and obscure.

The other part of oratory is to speak common things ingeniously or wittily, there being no little vigour and force added to words, when they are delivered in a neat and fine way, and somewhat out of the ordinary road, common and dull language relishing more of the clown than the gentleman. But herein also affectation must be avoided; it being better for a man by a native and clear eloquence to express himself, than by those words which may smell either of the lamp or ink-horn; so that, in general, one may observe that men who fortify and uphold their speeches with strong and evident reasons, have ever operated more on the minds of the auditors, than those who have made rhetorical excursions.

It will be better for a man who is doubtful of his pay to take an ordinary silver piece with its due stamp upon it, than an extraordinary gilded piece, which may perchance contain a baser metal under it; and perefer a well-flavoured wholesome woman, though with a tawny complexion, before a besmeared and painted face.

It is a general note, that a man's wit is best shewed in his answer, and his valour in his defence; that therefore as men learn in fencing how to ward all blows and thrusts which are or can be made against him, so it will be fitting to debate and resolve before-hand what you are to say or do upon any affront given you, least otherwise you should be surprised. Aristotle hath written a book of rhetoric, a work in my opinion not inferior to his best pieces, whom therefore with Cicero de Oratore, as also Quintilian, you may read for your instruction how to speak, neither of which two yet I can think so exact in their orations, but that a middle style will be of more efficacy, Cicero in my opinion being too long and tedious, and Quintilian too short and concise.

Having thus by moral philosophy enabled yourself to all that wisdom and goodness which is requisite to direct you in all your particular actions, it will be fit now to think how you are to behave yourself as a public person, or member of the commonwealth and kingdom wherein you live; as also to look into those principles and grounds upon which government is framed, it being manifest in nature that the wise doth easily govern the foolish, and the strong master the weak; so that he that could attain most wisdom and power, would quickly rule his fellows; for proof whereof, one may observe that a king is sick during that time the physicians govern him, and in day of battle an expert general appoints the king a place in which he shall stand, which was anciently the office of the constables de France. In law also, the judge is in a sort superior to his king, as long as he judgeth betwixt him and his people. In divinity also, he to whom the king commits the charge of his conscience, is his superior in that particular. All which instances may sufficiently prove, that in many cases the wiser governs or commands one less wise than himself, unless a wilful obstinacy be interposed; in which case recourse must be had to strength where obedience is necessary.

The exercises I chiefly used, and most recommend to my posterity, were riding the great horse and fencing, in which arts I had excellent masters, English, French, and Italian; as for dancing, I could never find leisure enough to learn it, as employing my mind always in acquiring of some art or science more useful; howbeit, I shall wish these three exercises learned in this order.

That dancing may be learned first, as that which doth fashion the body, gives one a good presence in and address to all companies, since it disposeth the limbs to a kind of *souplesse* (as the Frenchmen call it) and agility, insomuch as they seem to have the use of their legs, arms, and bodies, more than any others, who, standing stiff and stark in their postures, seem as if they were taken in their joints, or had not the perfect use of their members. I speak not this yet as if I would have a youth never stand still in company, but only that, when he hath occasion to stir, his motions may be comely and graceful; that he may learn to know how to come in and go out of a room where company is; how to make courtesies handsomely, according to the several degrees of persons he shall encounter; how to put off and hold his hat; all which, and many other things which become men, are taught by the more accurate dancing-masters in France.

The next exercise a young man should learn (but
not before he is eleven or twelve years of age) is
fencing; for the attaining of which the Frenchman's
rule is excellent, *bon pied bon œil*, by which to teach
men how far they may stretch out their feet when
they would make a thrust against their enemy, lest
either should overstride themselves, or not striding
far enough, fail to bring the point of their weapon
home: the second part of his direction adviseth the
scholar to keep a fixed eye upon the point of his
enemy's sword, to the intent he may both put by or
ward the blows and thrusts made against him, and
together direct the point of his sword upon some part
of his enemy that lieth naked and open to him.

The good fencing-masters, in France especially,
when they present a foil or *fleuret* to their scholars,
tell him it hath two parts, one of which he calleth
the *fort*, or strong, and the other the *faible*, or weak.
With the fort or strong, which extends from the
part of the hilt next the sword about a third part
of the whole length, thereof he teacheth his scholars
to defend themselves, and put by and ward the
thrusts and blows of his enemy, and with the other
two third parts to strike or thrust, as he shall see occasion; which rule also teacheth how to strike or thrust
high or low as his enemy doth, and briefly to take his
measure and time upon his adversary's motions,
whereby he may both defend himself or offend his
adversary, of which I have had much experiment and
use, both in the fleuret, or foil, as also when I fought
in good earnest with many persons at one and the

same time, as will appear in the sequel of my life.

And, indeed, I think I shall not speak vain-gloriously of myself, if I say, that no man understood the use of his weapon better than I did, or hath more dexterously prevailed himself thereof on all occasions ; since I found no man could be hurt but through some error in fencing.

I spent much time also in learning to ride the great horse,[1] that creature being made above all others for the service of man, as giving his rider all the advantages of which he is capable, while sometimes he gives him strength, sometimes agility or motion, for the overcoming of his enemy, insomuch that a good rider on a good horse, is as much above himself and others, as this world can make him. The rule for graceful riding is, that a man hold his eyes always betwixt the two ears, and his rod over the left ear of his horse, which he is to use for turning him every way, helping himself with his left foot, and rod upon the left part of his neck, to make his horse turn on the right hand, and with the right foot and help of his rod also (if needs be), to turn him on the left hand ; but this is to be used rather when one would make a horse understand these motions, than when he is a ready horse, the foot and stirrup alone applied to a either shoulder being sufficient, with the help of the reins, to make him turn any way. That a rider thus may have the use of his sword, or when it is requisite

---

[1] The horse of exceptional size and strength used in war.

only to make a horse go sidewards, it will be enough to keep the reins equal in his hand, and with the flat of his leg and foot together, and a touch upon the shoulder of the horse with the stirrup, to make him go sideward either way, without either advancing forward or returning backwards.

The most useful *air*, as the Frenchmen term it, is *terre-à-terre ;* the *courbettes, cabrioles,* or *un pas et un saut,*[1] being fitter for horses of parade and triumph than for soldiers ; yet I cannot deny but a *demivolte* with *courbettes,* so that they be not too high, may be useful in a fight or *mêlée,* for, as Labroue hath it in his book of horsemanship, Monsieur de Montmorency having a horse that was excellent in performing the demivolte, did with his sword strike down two adversaries from their horses in a tourney, where divers of the prime gallants of France did meet ; for taking his time when the horse was in the height of his courbette, and discharging a blow, then his sword fell with such weight and force upon the two cavaliers one after another, that he struck them from their horses to the ground.

The manner of fighting a duel on horseback I was taught thus : we had each of us a reasonable stiff riding-rod in our hands, about the length of a sword, and so rid one against the other ; he, as the more expert, sat still to pass me, and then to get behind me, and after to turn with his right hand upon my left side with his rod, that so he might hit me with the

---

[1] Terms of horsemanship for different leaps.

point thereof in the body ; and he that can do this handsomely, is sure to overcome his adversary, it being impossible to bring his sword about enough to defend himself or offend the assailant ; and to get this advantage, which they call in French *gagner la croupe*, nothing is so useful as to make a horse to go only sideward until his adversary be past him, since he will by this means avoid his adversary's blow or thrust, and on a sudden get on the left hand of his adversary, in the manner I formerly related. But of this art let Labroue and Pluvinel[1] be read, who are excellent masters in that art, of whom I must confess I learned much ; though, to speak ingeniously, my breaking two or three colts, and teaching them after-wards those *airs* of which they were most capable, taught me both what I was to do, and made me see mine errors, more than all their precepts.

To make a horse fit for the wars, and embolden him against all terrors, these inventions are useful : to beat a drum out of the stable first, and then give him his provender, then beat a drum in the stable by degrees, and then give him his provender upon the drum. When he is acquainted herewith sufficiently, you must shoot off a pistol out of the stable, before he hath his provender ; then you may shoot off a pistol in the stable, and so by degrees bring it as near

---

[1] Antoine de Pluvinel, Master of Horse to Louis XIII., published a folio entitled, *Instruction du Roi en l'exercise de monter à cheval.* Paris, 1619. It consists of dialogues between the young King, the Duc de Bellegarde, and himself ; with cuts by Crispin Pass, exhibiting the system of the manège. Labroue, also an author on equitation.

to him as you can till he be acquainted with the pistol, likewise remembering still after every shot to give him more provender. You must also cause his groom to put on bright armour, and so to rub his heels and dress him; you must also present a sword before him in the said armour, and when you have done, give him still some more provender. Lastly, his rider must bring his horse forth into the open field, where a bright armour must be fastened upon a stake, and set forth in the likeness of an armed man as much as possible; which being done, the rider must put his horse on till he make him not only approach the said image, but throw it down; which being done, you must be sure to give him some provender, that he may be encouraged to do the like against an adversary in battle. It will be good also that two men do hold up a cloak betwixt them in the field, and then the rider to put the horse to it till he leap over, which cloak also they may raise as they see occasion, when the horse is able to leap so high. You shall do well also to use your horse to swimming, which you may do either by trailing him after you at the tail of a boat, in a good river, holding him by the head at the length of the bridle, or by putting a good swimmer, in a linen waistcoat and breeches, upon him.

It will be fit for a gentleman also to learn to swim, unless he be given to cramps and convulsions; howbeit, I must confess, in my own particular, that I cannot swim, for as I was once in danger of drowning by learning to swim, my mother upon her blessing charged me never to learn swimming, telling me

farther, that she had heard of more drowned than
saved by it; which reason, though it did not prevail
with me, yet her commandment did. It will be good
also for a gentleman to learn to leap, wrestle, and
vault on horseback, they being all of them qualities of
great use. I do much approve likewise of shooting
in the long bow, as being both an healthful exercise,
and useful for the wars, notwithstanding all that our
firemen speak against it; for, bring a hundred archers
against so many musqueteers, I say if the archer
comes within his distance, he will not only make two
shoots, but two hits for one.

The exercises I do not approve of are riding of
running horses,[1] there being much cheating in that
kind; neither do I see why a brave man should
delight in a creature whose chief use is to help him to
run away. I do not much like of hunting horses,
that exercise taking up more time than can be spared
from a man studious to get knowledge; it is enough,
therefore, to know the sport, if there be any in it,
without making it an ordinary practice; and indeed
of the two hawking is the better, because less time is
spent in it; and upon these terms also I can allow a
little bowling, so that the company be choice and good.

The exercises I wholly condemn, are dicing and
carding, especially if you play for any great sum of
money, or spend any time in them, or use to come to
meetings in dicing-houses, where cheaters meet and

---

[1] Newmarket, observes Mr. Lee, was acquiring its first fame in the
fashionable world when Lord Herbert was a young man.

cozen young gentlemen of all their money. I could say much more concerning all these points of education, and particularly concerning the discreet civility which is to be observed in communication either with friends or strangers, but this work would grow too big, and that many precepts conducing thereunto may be had in *Guazzo de la Civile Conversation* and *Galeteus de Moribus.*

It would also deserve a particular lecture or *recherche,* how one ought to behave himself with children, servants, tenants, and neighbours; and I am confident that precepts in this point will be found more useful to young gentlemen than all the subtelties of schools. I confess I have collected many things to this purpose, which I forbear to set down here, because (if God grant me life and health) I intend to make a little treatise concerning these points. I shall return now to the narration of mine own history.

When I had attained the age betwixt eighteen or nineteen years, my mother, together with myself and wife, removed up to London, where we took house, and kept a greater family than became either my mother's widow's estate, or such young beginners as we were, especially since six brothers and three sisters were to be provided for, my father having made either no will, or such an imperfect one, that it was not proved. My mother, although she had all my father's leases and goods, which were of great value, yet she desired me to undertake that burden of providing for my brothers and sisters, which, to gratify my mother, as well as those so near me, I was voluntarily content to provide thus far, as to give my six brothers thirty pounds apiece yearly, during their lives, and my sisters one thousand pounds apiece, which portions married them to those I have above mentioned. My younger sister, indeed, might have been married to a far greater fortune, had not the overthwartness of some neighbours interrupted it.

About the year of our Lord 1600, I came to London, shortly after which the attempt of the Earl of Essex, related in our history, followed, which I had rather were seen in the writers of that argument than here. Not long after this, curiosity, rather than ambition, brought me to court; and, as it was the manner of those times for all men to kneel down before the great Queen Elizabeth, who then reigned, I was likewise upon my knees in the presence-chamber, when she passed by to the chapel at Whitehall. As soon as she saw me she stopped, and swearing her usual oath,[1] demanded, "Who is this?" Everybody there present looked upon me, but no man knew me, until Sir James Croft, a pensioner, finding the queen stayed, returned back and told who I was, and that I had married Sir William Herbert of St. Julian's daughter. The queen hereupon looked attentively upon me, and swearing again her ordinary oath, said, "It is pity he was married so young;" and thereupon gave her hand to kiss twice, both times gently clapping me on the cheek. I remember little more of myself, but that from that time until King James's coming to

---

[1] " God's death ! "

the crown, I had a son, which died shortly afterwards, and that I attended my studies seriously, the more I learnt out of my books adding still a desire to know more.

King James being now acknowledged king, and coming towards London, I thought fit to meet his majesty at Burleigh, near Stamford. Shortly after I was made Knight of the Bath, with the usual ceremonies belonging to that ancient order. I could tell how much my person was commended by the lords and ladies that came to see the solemnity then used, but I shall flatter myself too much if I believed it.

I must not forget yet the ancient custom, being that some principal person was to put on the right spur of those the king had appointed to receive that dignity. The Earl of Shrewsbury seeing my esquire there with my spur in his hand, voluntarily came to me and said, "Cousin, I believe you will be a good knight, and therefore I will put on your spur;" whereupon after my most humble thanks for so great a favour, I held up my leg against the wall, and he put on my spur.

There is another custom likewise, that the knights the first day wear the gown of some religious order, and the night following to be bathed; after which they take an oath never to sit in place where injustice should be done, but they shall right it to the uttermost of their power; and particularly ladies and gentlewomen that shall be wronged in their honour, if they demand assistance, and many other points, not unlike the romances of knight errantry.

The second day to wear robes of crimson taffety (in which habit I am painted in my study), and so to ride from St. James's to Whitehall, with our esquires before us; and the third day to wear a gown of purple satin, upon the left sleeve whereof is fastened certain strings weaved of white silk and gold tied in a knot, and tassels to it of the same, which all the knights are obliged to wear until they have done something famous in arms, or until some lady of honour take it off, and fasten it on her sleeve, saying, I will answer he shall prove a good knight. I had not long worn this string, but a principal lady of the court, and certainly, in most men's opinion, the handsomest,[1] took mine off, and said she would pledge her honour for mine. I do not name this lady, because some passages happened afterwards, which oblige me to silence, though nothing could be justly said to her prejudice or wrong.

Shortly after this I intended to go with Charles, Earl of Nottingham, the Lord Admiral, who went to Spain to take the king's oath for confirmation of the articles of peace betwixt the two crowns; howbeit, by the industry of some near me, who desired to stay

---

[1] It is uncertain who this lady was; but there is no doubt of her being the same person mentioned afterwards, whom he calls *the fairest of her time*. Perhaps, conjecturing from a passage of Selden, Lady Kent. "Lady Kent articled with Sir Edward Herbert that he should come to her when she sent for him, and stay with her as long as she would have him, to which he set his hand; then he articled with her that he should go away when he pleased, and stay away as long as he pleased, to which she set her hand."

me at home, I was hindered, and instead of going that voyage, was made Sheriff of Montgomeryshire, concerning which I will say no more, but that I bestowed the place of under-sheriff, as also other places in my gifts freely, without either taking gift or reward ; which custom also I have observed throughout the whole course of my life ; insomuch that when I was ambassador in France, and might have had great presents, which former ambassadors accepted, for doing lawful courtesies to merchants and others, yet no gratuity, upon what terms soever, could ever be fastened upon me.

This public duty did not hinder me yet to follow my beloved studies in a country life for the most part ; although sometimes also I resorted to court, without yet that I had any ambition there, and much less was tainted with those corrupt delights incident to the times ; for, living with my wife in all conjugal loyalty for the space of about ten years after my marriage, I wholly declined the allurements and temptations whatsoever, which might incline me to violate my marriage bed.

About the year 1608, my two daughters, called Beatrice, and Florence who lived not yet long after, and one son Richard being born, and come to so much maturity, that, though in their mere childhood, they gave no little hopes of themselves for the future time, I called them all before my wife, demanding how she liked them, to which she answering, "Well;" I demanded then, whether she was willing to do so much for them as I would ? Whereupon she, replying, demanded what I meant by that. I told her, that for my part I was but young for a man, and she not old for a woman; that our lives were in the hands of God; that, if He pleased to call either of us away, that party which remained might marry again, and have children by some other, to which our estates might be disposed; for preventing whereof I thought fit to motion to her, that if she would assure upon the son any quantity of lands from three hundred pounds a year to one thousand I would do the like. But my wife not approving hereof, answered in these express words, that she would not draw the cradle upon her head; whereupon, I desiring her to advise better upon the business, and to take some few days' respite for that purpose, she seemed to depart from me not very well contented.

About a week or ten days afterwards, I demanded again what she thought concerning the motion I made, to which yet she said no more, but that she thought she had already answered me sufficiently to the point. I told her then, that I should make another motion to her, which was, that in regard I was too young to go beyond sea before I married her, she now would give me leave for a while to see foreign countries; howbeit, if she would assure her lands as I would mine, in the manner above mentioned, I would never depart from her. She answered, that I knew her mind before concerning that point, yet that she should be sorry I went beyond sea, nevertheless, if I would needs go, she could not help it.

This, whether a licence taken or given, served my turn to prepare without delay, for a journey beyond sea, that so I might satisfy that curiosity I long since had to see foreign countries. So that I might leave my wife so little discontented as I could, I left her not only posterity to renew the family of the Herberts of St. Julian's, according to her father's desire, to inherit his lands, but the rents of all the lands she brought with her, reserving mine own partly to pay my brothers' and sisters' portions, and defraying my charges abroad. Upon which terms, though I was sorry to leave my wife, as having lived most honestly with her all this time, I thought it no such unjust ambition to attain the knowledge of foreign countries, especially since I had in great part already attained the languages, and that I intended not to spend any long time out of my country.

Before I departed yet, I left her with child of a son, christened afterwards by the name of Edward; and now coming to court, I obtained a license to go beyond sea, taking with me for my companion Mr. Aurelian Townsend,[1] a gentleman that spoke the languages of French, Italian, and Spanish in great perfection, and a man to wait in my chamber, who spoke French, two lackeys, and three horses. Coming thus to Dover, and passing the seas thence to Calais, I journeyed without any memorable adventure, till I came to Faubourg St. Germain, in Paris, where Sir George

---

[1] Wrote *Albion's Triumph* and *Temps Restored.* Masques, both published London, 1631.

Carew, then ambassador for the king, lived; I was kindly received by him, and often invited to his table.

Next to his house dwelt the Duke of Vantadour, who had married a daughter of Monsieur de Montmorency, Grand Constable de France. Many visits being exchanged between that Duchess and the lady of our ambassador, it pleased the duchess to invite me to her father's house, at the castle of Merlou,[1] being about twenty-four miles from Paris; and here I found much welcome from that brave old general,[2] who being informed of my name, said he knew well of what family I was; telling, the first notice he had of the Herberts was at the siege of St. Quintin, where my grandfather, with a command of foot under William Earl of Pembroke, was. Passing two or three days here, it happened one evening that a daughter of the duchess, of about ten or eleven years of age, going one evening from the castle to walk in the meadows, myself, with divers French gentlemen, attended her and some gentlewomen that were with her. This young lady wearing a knot of riband on her head, a French chevalier took it suddenly, and fastened it to his hatband. The young lady, offended herewith, demands her riband, but he refusing to restore it, the young

---

[1] Now called Mello, not far from Clermont (Oise). *On y admire encore un château, un parc, et un domaine magnifiques.*—DE RÉMUSAT.

[2] Henri de Montmorency, second son of the Constable Anne de Montmorency, killed at the battle of St. Denis, 1567. Henri de Montmorency was made constable by Henri IV. The Duchess of Vantadour, mentioned above, was Margaret, second daughter of the constable, and wife of Anne de Levi, Duke of Vantadour.

lady addressing herself to me, said, " Monsieur, I pray
get my riband from that gentleman " ; hereupon going
towards him, I courteously, with my hat in my hand,
desired him to do me the honour, that I may deliver
the lady her riband or bouquet again ; but he roughly
answering me, " Do you think I will give it you,
when I have refused it to her ? " I replied, " Nay
then, sir, I will make you restore it by force ; "
whereupon also, putting on my hat and reaching at
his, he to save himself ran away, and, after a long
course in the meadow, finding that I had almost
overtook him, he turned short, and running to the
young lady, was about to put the riband on her hand,
when I, seizing upon his arm, said to the young lady,
" It was I that gave it." " Pardon me," quoth she,
" it is he that gives it me." I said then, " Madam, I
will not contradict you, but if he dare say that I did
not constrain him to give it, I will fight with him."
The French gentleman answered nothing thereunto
for the present, and so conducted the young lady
again to the castle. The next day I desired Mr.
Aurelian Townsend to tell the French cavalier, that
either he must confess that I constrained him to
restore the riband, or fight with me ; but the gentleman seeing him unwilling to accept of this challenge,
went out from the place, whereupon I following him,
some of the gentlemen that belonged to the constable
taking notice hereof, acquainted him therewith,
who sending for the French cavalier, checked him
well for his sauciness, in taking the riband away from
his grandchild, and afterwards bid him depart his

house ; and this was all that I ever heard of the gentleman, with whom I proceeded in that manner, because I thought myself obliged thereunto by the oath taken when I was made Knight of the Bath, as I formerly related upon this occasion.

I must remember also, that three other times I engaged myself to challenge men to fight with me, who I conceived had injured ladies and gentlewomen ; one was in defence of my cousin Sir Francis Newport's daughter, who was married to John Barker, of Hamon, whose younger brother and heir[1] . . . . sent him a challenge, which to this day he never answered, and would have beaten him afterwards, but that I was hindered by my uncle Sir Francis Newport.

I had another occasion to challenge one Captain Vaughan, who I conceived offered some injury to my sister the Lady Jones of Abermarles. I sent him a challenge, which he accepted, the place between us being appointed beyond Greenwich, with seconds on both sides. Hereupon I coming to the King's Head, in Greenwich, with intention the next morning to be in the place, I found the house beset with at least a hundred persons, partly sent by the Lords of the Privy Council, who gave order to apprehend me.

I hearing thereof, desired my servant to bring my horses as far as he could from my lodging, but yet within sight of me ; which being done, and all this company coming to lay hold on me, I and my second, who was my cousin James Price of Hanachly, sallied

---

[1] The text here lacks continuity.

out of the doors, with our swords drawn, and in spite of that multitude made our way to our horses, where my servant very honestly opposing himself against those who would have laid hands upon us, while we got upon horseback, was himself laid hold on by them, and evil treated ; which I perceiving, rid back again, and with my sword in my hand rescued him, and afterwards seeing him get on horseback, charged them to go anywhere rather than to follow me. Riding afterwards with my second to the place appointed, I found nobody there, which, as I heard afterwards, happened, because the Lords of the Council taking notice of this difference, apprehended him, and charged him in his Majesty's name not to fight with me ; since otherwise I believed he would not have failed.

The third that I questioned in this kind was a Scotch gentleman, who taking a riband in the like manner from Mrs. Middlemore, a maid of honour, as was done from the young lady above mentioned, in a back room behind Queen Anne's lodgings in Greenwich, she likewise desired me to get her the said riband. I repaired, as formerly, to him in a courteous manner to demand it, but he refusing as the French cavalier did, I caught him by the neck, and had almost thrown him down, when company came in and parted us. I offered likewise to fight with this gentleman, and came to the place appointed by Hyde Park ; but this also was interrupted by order of the Lords of the Council, and I never heard more of him.

These passages, though different in time, I have related here together, both for the similitude of argument, and that it may appear how strictly I held myself to my oath of knighthood; since for the rest I can truly say, that though I have lived in the armies and courts of the greatest princes in Christendom, yet I never had a quarrel with man for mine own sake; so that, although in mine own nature I was ever choleric and hasty, yet I never, without occasion given, quarrelled with any body, and as little did any body attempt to give me offence, as having as clear a reputation for my courage as whosoever of my time. For my friends often I have hazarded myself, but never yet drew my sword for my own sake singly, as hating ever the doing of injury, contenting myself only to resent them when they were offered me. After this digression I shall return to my history.

That brave Constable in France testifying now more than formerly his regard of me, at his departure from Merlou to his fair house at Chantilly, five or six miles distant, said he left that castle to be commanded by me, as also his forests and chases, which were well stored with wild boar and stag, and that I might hunt them when I pleased. He told me also, that if I would learn to ride the great horse, he had a stable there of some fifty, the best and choicest as was thought in France; and that his écuyer, called Monsieur de Disancourt, not inferior to Pluvenal[1] or

---

[1] Pluvenal was first Master of the Horse to Henri III., rose to be Ambassador to Holland under Henri IV.; he wrote *Le Manège Royal,* edited by Réne de Menou, probably the M. de Mennou mentioned by Lord Herbert. Pluvenal is regarded as the founder of riding schools.—DE RÉMUSAT.

Labroue, should teach me. I did with great thankfulness accept his offer, as being very much addicted to the exercise of riding great horses; and as for hunting in his forests, I told him I should use it sparingly, as being desirous to preserve his game. He commanded also his écuyer to keep a table for me, and his pages to attend me, the chief of whom was Monsieur de Mennon, who, proving to be one of the best horsemen in France, keeps now an academy in Paris. And here I shall recount a little passage betwixt him and his master, that the inclination of the French at that time may appear; there being scarce any man thought worth the looking on, that had not killed some other in duel.

Mennon desiring to marry a niece of Monsieur Disancourt, who it was thought should be his heir, was thus answered by him: " Friend, it is not time yet to marry; I will tell you what you must do. If you will be a brave man, you must first kill in single combat two or three men, then afterwards marry and engender two or three children, or the world will neither have got nor lost by you;" of which strange counsel, Disancourt was no otherwise the author than as he had been an example, at least of the former part; it being his fortune to have fought three or four brave duels in his time.

And now, as every morning I mounted the great horse, so in the afternoons I many times went a-hunting, the manner of which was this. The Duke of Montmorency having given orders to the tenants of the town of Merlou, and some villages adjoining, to attend me when I went a-hunting, they, upon my summons, usually repaired to those woods where I intended to find my game, with drums and muskets, to the number of sixty or eighty, and sometimes one hundred or more persons; they entering the wood on that side with that noise, discharging their pieces and beating their drums, we on the other side of the wood having placed mastiffs and greyhounds, to the number of twenty or thirty, which Monsieur de Montmorency kept near his castle, expected those beasts they should force out of the wood. If stags or wild boars came forth, we commonly spared them, pursuing only the wolves, which were there in great number, of which are found two sorts; the mastiff wolf, thick and short, though he could not indeed run fast, yet would fight with our dogs; the greyhound wolf, long and swift, who many times escaped our best dogs, though when he were overtaken, easily killed by us, without making much resistance. Of both these sorts I killed divers with my sword, while I stayed here.

One time also it was my fortune to kill a wild boar in this manner. The boar being roused from his den, fled before our dogs for a good space; but finding them press him hard, turned his head against our dogs, and hurt three or four of them very dangerously. I came on horseback up to him, and with my sword thrust him twice or thrice without entering his skin, the blade being not so stiff as it should be.

The boar hereupon turned upon me, and much endangered my horse, which I perceiving, rid a little out of the way, and leaving my horse with my lackey, returned with my sword against the boar, who by this time had hurt more dogs ; and here happened a pretty kind of fight, for when I thrust at the boar sometimes with my sword, which in some places I made enter, the boar would run at me, whose tusks yet by stepping a little out of the way I avoided, but he then turning upon me, the dogs came in, and drew him off, so that he fell upon them, which I perceiving, ran at the boar with my sword again, which made him turn upon me, but then the dogs pulled him from me again, while so relieving one another by turns, we killed the boar.

At this chase Monsieur Disancourt and Mennon were present, as also Mr. Townsend, yet so as they did endeavour rather to withdraw me from than assist me in the danger. Of which boar, some part being well seasoned and larded, I presented to my uncle Sir Francis Newport in Shropshire, and found most excellent meat.

Thus having passed a whole summer, partly in these exercises, and partly in visits of the Duke of Montmorency, at his fair house in Chantilly, which, for its extraordinary fairness and situation, I shall here describe.

A little river descending from some higher grounds, in a country which was almost all his own, and falling at last upon a rock in the middle of a valley, which, to keep its way forwards, it must on one or other side thereof have declined. Some of the ancestors of the Montmorencies, to ease the river of this labour, made divers channels through this rock, to give it a free passage, dividing the rock by that means into little islands, upon which he built a great strong castle, joined together with bridges, and sumptuously furnished with hangings of silk and gold, rare pictures and statues; all which buildings united, as I formerly told, were encompassed about with water, which was paved with stone (those which were used in the building of the house were drawn from thence). One might see the huge carps, pike, and trouts, which were kept in several divisions, gliding along the waters very easily. Yet nothing in my opinion added so much to the glory of this castle, as a forest adjoining close to it, and upon a level with the house; for being of a very large extent, and set thick both with tall trees and underwood, the whole forest, which was replenished with wild boar, stag, and roe-deer, was cut out into long walks every way, so that, although the dogs might follow their chase through the thickets, the huntsmen might ride along the said walks, and meet or overtake their game in some one of them, they being cut with that art, that they led to all the parts in the said forest. And here also I have hunted the wild boar divers times, both then and afterwards, when his son, the Duke of Montmorency, succeeded him in the possession of that incomparable place.

And there I cannot but remember the direction the old Constable gave me to return to his castle out of this admirable labyrinth; telling me, I should look upon what side the trees were roughest and hardest, which being found, I might be confident that part stood northward, which being observed, I might easily find the east, as being on the right hand, and so guide my way home.

How much this house, together with the forest, hath been valued by great princes, may appear by two little narratives I shall here insert. Charles V. the great emperor, passing in the time of François I. from Spain into the Low Countries, by the way of France, was entertained for some time in this house by a Duke of Montmorency, who was likewise Constable de France, after he had taken this palace into his consideration, with the forests adjoining, said he would willingly give one of his provinces for such a place, there being, as he thought, nowhere such a situation.

Henry IV. also was desirous of this house, and offered to exchange any of his houses, with much more lands than his estate thereabouts was worth; to which the Duke of Montmorency made this wary answer: '*Sieur, la maison est à vous, mais que je sois le concierge;*' which in English sounds thus: "Sir, the house is yours, but give me leave to keep it for you."

When I had been at Merlou about eight months, and attained, as was thought, the knowledge of horsemanship, I came to the Duke of Montmorency at Chantilly, and, after due thanks for his favours, took my leave of him to go to Paris; whereupon the good old prince embracing me, and calling me son, bid me farewell, assuring me nevertheless he should be glad of any occasion hereafter to testify his love and esteem for me; telling me farther, he should come to Paris himself shortly, where he hoped to see me. From hence I returned to Merlou, where I gave Monsieur Disancourt such a present as abundantly requited the charges of my diet, and the pains of his teaching. Being now ready to set forth, a gentleman from the Duke of Montmorency came to me, and told me his master would not let me go without giving me a present, which I might keep as an earnest of his affection; whereupon also a genet, for which the duke had sent expressly into Spain, and which cost him there five hundred crowns, as I were told, was brought to me. The greatness of this gift, together with other courtesies received, did not a little trouble me, as not knowing then how to requite them. I would have given my horses I had there, which were of great value, to him, but that I thought them too mean a present; but the duke also suspecting that I meant to do so, prevented me, saying, that as I loved him, I should think upon no requital while I stayed in France, but when I came into England, if I sent him a mare that ambled naturally, I should much gratify him. I told the messenger I should strive, both that way and every way else, to declare my thankfulness, and so dismissed the messenger with a good reward.

Coming now to Paris, through the recommendation of the lord ambassador, I was received to the house of that incomparable scholar Isaac Casaubon, by whose learned conversation I much benefited myself; besides, I did apply myself much to know the use of my arms, and to ride the great horse, playing on the lute, and singing according to the rules of the French masters.

Sometimes also I went to the court of the French king, Henry IV., who, upon information of me in the garden at the Tuileries, received me with all courtesy, embracing me in his arms, and holding me some while there. I went sometimes also to the court of Queen Margaret, at the hostel, called by her name; and here I saw many balls or masks, in all which it pleased that Queen publicly to place me next to her chair, not without the wonder of some, and the envy of another, who was wont to have that favour. I shall recount one accident which happened while I was there.

All things being ready for the ball, and every one being in their place, and I myself next to the Queen, expecting when the dancers would come in, one knocked at the door somewhat louder than became, as I thought, a very civil person. When he came in, I remember there was a sudden whisper among the ladies, saying, "*C'est Monsieur Balagny,*" or, "It is Monsieur Balagny:"[1] whereupon also I saw the ladies and gentlewomen, one after another, invite him to sit near them, and, which is more, when one lady had his company a while, another would say, "You have

---

[1] Damien de Montluc, Seigneur de Balagny, son of the Marshal of France of this name, and nephew of Bussy d'Amboise of Chapman fame.

enjoyed him long enough, I must have him now;" at which bold civility of theirs, though I were astonished, yet it added unto my wonder, that his person could not be thought at most but ordinary handsome; his hair, which was cut very short, half grey, his doublet but of sackcloth cut to his shirt, and his breeches only of plain grey cloth. Informing myself by some standers-by who he was, I was told that he was one of the gallantest men in the world, as having killed eight or nine men in single fight, and that for this reason the ladies made so much of him, it being the manner of all Frenchwomen to cherish gallant men, as thinking they could not make so much of any else with the safety of their honour. This cavalier, though his head was half grey, he had not yet attained the age of thirty years, whom I have thought fit to remember more particularly here, because of some passages that happened afterwards betwixt him and me, at the siege of Juliers, as I shall tell in its place.

Having past thus all the winter, until about the latter end of January,[1] without any such memorable accident as I shall think fit to set down particularly, I took my leave of the French king, Queen Margaret, and the nobles and ladies in both courts; at which time the Princess of Conti desired me to carry a scarf into England, and present it to Queen Anne on her part, which being accepted, myself and Sir Thomas Lucy[2] (whose second I had been twice in France,

---

[1] 1609. *Lee.*

[2] Eldest son of the Sir Thomas Lucy of Shaksperean biography. — See *Lee.*

against two cavaliers of our nation, who yet were hindered to fight with us in the field, where we attended them), we came on our way as far as Dieppe, in Normandy, and there took ship about the beginning of February, when so furious a storm arose, that with very great danger we were at sea all night.

The master of our ship lost both the use of his compass and his reason; for not knowing whither he was carried by the tempest, all the help he had was by the lightnings, which, together with thunder very frequently that night, terrified him, yet gave the advantage sometimes to discover whether we were upon our coast, to which he thought, by the course of his glasses, we were near approached. And now towards day we found ourselves, by great providence of God, within view of Dover, to which the master of our ship did make. The men of Dover rising betimes in the morning, to see whether any ship were coming towards them, were in great numbers upon the shore, as believing the tempest, which had thrown down barns and trees near the town, might give them the benefit of some wreck, if perchance any ship were driven thitherwards.

We coming thus in extreme danger, straight upon the pier of Dover, which stands out in the sea, our ship was unfortunately split against it; the master said, *Mes amis, nous sommes perdus;* or, My friends, we are cast away; when myself, who heard the ship crack against the pier, and then found, by the master's words, it was time for every one to save themselves, if they could, got out of my cabin (though very sea-sick), and climbing up the mast a little way, drew my sword and flourished it. They at Dover having the sign given them, adventured in a shallop of six oars to relieve us, which being come with great danger to the side of our ship, I got into it first, with my sword in my hand, and called for Sir Thomas Lucy, saying, that if any man offered to get in before him, I should resist him with my sword; whereupon, a faithful servant of his taking Sir Thomas Lucy out of the cabin, who was half-dead of sea-sickness, put him into my arms, whom after I had received, I bid the shallop make away for shore, and the rather, that I saw another shallop coming to relieve us; when a post from France, who carried letters, finding the ship still rent more and more, adventured to leap from the top of our ship into the shallop, where, falling fortunately on some of the stronger timber of the boat, and not on the planks, which he must needs have broken, and so sunk us, had he fallen upon them, escaped together with us two, unto the land. I must confess, myself as also the seamen that were in the shallop, thought once to have killed him for this desperate attempt; but finding no harm followed, we escaped together unto the land, from whence we sent more shallops, and so made means to save both men and horses that were in the ship, which yet itself was wholly split and cast away, insomuch that, in pity to the master, Sir Thomas Lucy and myself gave thirty pounds towards his loss, which yet was not so great as we thought, since the tide now ebbing, he recovered the broken parts of his ship.

Coming thus to London, and afterwards to court, I kissed his majesty's hand, and acquainted him with some particulars concerning France. As for the present I had to deliver to her majesty from the Princess of Conti, I thought fit rather to send it by one of the ladies that attended her, than to presume to demand audience of her in person. But her majesty not satisfied herewith, commanded me to attend her, and demanded divers questions of me concerning that princess and the courts in France, saying she would speak more at large with me at some other time ; for which purpose she commanded me to wait on her often, wishing me to advise her what present she might return back again.

Howbeit, not many weeks after, I returned to my wife and family again, where I passed some time, partly in my studies, and partly riding the great horse, of which I had a stable well furnished. No horse yet was so dear to me as the genet I brought from France, whose love I had so gotten, that he would suffer none else to ride him, nor indeed any man to come near him, when I was upon him, as being in his nature a most furious horse. His true picture may be seen in the chapel chamber in my house, where I am painted riding him, and this motto by me :

Me totum bonitas bonum suprema
Reddas ; me intrepidum dabo vel ipse.

This horse, as soon as ever I came to the stable, would neigh, and when I drew near him would lick my hand, and (when I suffered him) my cheek, but yet would permit nobody to come near his heels at the same time. Sir Thomas Lucy would have given me two hundred pounds for this horse, which, though I would not accept, yet I left the horse with him when I went to the Low Countries, who not long after died. The occasion of my going thither was thus. Hearing that a war about the title of Cleve, Juliers, and some other provinces betwixt the Low Countries and Germany, should be made, by the several pretenders to it, and that the French king himself would come with a great army into those parts; it was now the year of our Lord 1610, when my Lord Chandos[1] and myself resolved to take shipping for the Low Countries, and from thence to pass to the city of Juliers, which the Prince of Orange resolved to besiege. Making all haste thither, we found the siege newly begun; the Low Country army assisted by 4000 English, under the command of Sir Edward Cecil. We had not been long there, when the Marshal de la Chastre, instead of Henry IV., who was killed by that villain Ravaillac, came with a brave French army thither, in which Monsieur Balagny I formerly mentioned was a colonel.

My Lord Chandos lodged himself in the quarters where Sir Horace Vere was; I went and quartered with Sir Edward Cecil, where I was lodged next to him in a hut I made there, going yet both by day and night to the trenches, we making our approaches to the town on one side, and the French on the

---

[1] Grey Bridges, Lord Chandos, made Knight of the Bath in 1604. He was dubbed for his hospitality and magnificence, the *King of Cotswold*.

other. Our lines were drawn towards the point of a bulwark of the citadel, or castle, thought to be one of the best fortifications in Christendom, and encompassed about with a deep wet ditch. We lost many men in making these approaches, the town and castle being very well provided both with great and small shot, and a garrison in it of about 4000 men, besides the burghers. Sir Edward Cecil (who was a very active general), used often during the siege, to go in person in the night time, to try whether he could catch any sentinels *perdus;* and for this purpose, still desired me to accompany him; in performing whereof, both of us did much hazard ourselves, for the first sentinel retiring to the second, and the second to the third, three shots were commonly made at us, before we could do anything, though afterwards chasing them with our swords almost home unto their guards, we had some sport in the pursuit of them.

One day Sir Edward Cecil and myself coming to the approaches that Monsieur de Balagny had made towards a bulwark or bastion of that city, Monsieur de Balagny, in the presence of Sir Edward Cecil and divers English and French captains then present, said *Monsieur, on dit que vous êtes un des plus braves de votre nation, et je suis Balagny, allons voir qui fera le mieux;* "They say, you are one of the bravest of your nation, and I am Balagny, let us see who will do best;" whereupon leaping suddenly out of the trenches with his sword drawn, I did in the like manner as suddenly follow him, both of us in the mean while striving who should be foremost, which being perceived by those of the bulwark and cortine opposite to us, three or four hundred shot at least, great and small, were made against us. Our running on forwards in emulation of each other, was the cause that all the shots fell betwixt us and the trench from which we sallied. When Monsieur Balagny, finding such a storm of bullets, said, *Pardieu, il fait bien chaud,* "It is very hot here;" I answered briefly thus, " *Vous en irez primier, autrement je n'irai jamais;*" "You shall go first or else I will never go;" hereupon he ran with all speed, and somewhat crouching towards the trenches, I followed after leisurely and upright, and yet came within the trenches before they on the bulwark or cortine could charge again. Which passage afterwards being related to the Prince of Orange, he said it was a strange bravado of Balagny, and that we went to an unavoidable death.

I could relate divers things of note concerning myself, during this siege, but do forbear, lest I should relish too much of vanity. It shall suffice that my passing over the ditch unto the wall, first of all the nations there, is set down by William Crofts,[1] M.A., and soldier, who hath written and printed the history of the Low Countries.

There happened during this siege a particular quarrel betwixt me and the Lord of Walden,[2] eldest

[1] Should be William Crosse, author of a continuation of a " General History of the Netherlands."—See *Lee.*

[2] Theophilus, Lord Howard of Walden, eldest son of Thomas Earl of Suffolk, whom he succeeded in the title, Knight of the Garter, Constable of Dover Castle, and captain of the Band of Pensioners.

son to the Earl of Suffolk, Lord Treasurer of England at that time, which I do but unwillingly relate, in regard of the great esteem I have of that noble family; howbeit, to avoid misreports, I have thought fit to set it down truly. That lord having been invited to a feast in Sir Horace Vere's quarters, where (after the Low Country manner) there was liberal drinking, returned not long after to Sir Edward Cecil's quarters, at which time, I speaking merrily to him, upon some slight occasion, he took that offence at me, which he would not have done at another time, insomuch that he came towards me in a violent manner, which I perceiving, did more than half way meet him; but the company were so vigilant upon us that before any blow past we were separated; howbeit, because he made towards me, I thought fit the next day to send him a challenge, telling him, that if he had any thing to say to me, I would meet him in such a place as no man should interrupt us. Shortly after this, Sir Thomas Peyton came to me on his part, and told me my lord would fight me on horseback with single sword; and, said he, " I will be his second; where is yours ?" I replied that neither his lordship nor myself brought over any great horses with us; that I knew he might much better borrow one than myself; howbeit, as soon as he shewed me the place, he should find me there on horseback or on foot; whereupon both of us riding together upon two geldings to the side of a wood, Peyton said he chose that place, and the time break of day the next morning. I told him, "I would fail neither place nor time, though I

knew not where to get a better horse than the nag
I rid on; and as for a second, I shall trust to your
nobleness, who, I know, will see fair play betwixt us,
though you come on his side." But he urging me again
to provide a second, I told him I could promise for
none but myself, and that if I spoke to any of my
friends in the army to this purpose, I doubted least
the business might be discovered and prevented.

He was no sooner gone from me, but night drew on,
myself resolving in the mean time to rest under a fair
oak all night; after this, tying my horse by the bridle
unto another tree, I had not now rested two hours, when
I found some fires nearer to me than I thought was
possible in so solitary a place, whereupon also having
the curiosity to see the reason hereof, I got on horseback again, and had not rode very far, when by the
talk of the soldiers there, I found I was in the Scotch
quarter, where finding in a stable a very fair horse of
service, I desired to know whether he might be
bought for any reasonable sum of money, but a soldier
replying it was their captain's, Sir James Areskin's
chief horse, I demanded for Sir James, but the soldier
answering he was not within the quarter, I demanded
then for his lieutenant, whereupon the soldier
courteously desired him to come to me. This
lieutenant was called Montgomery, and had the
reputation of a gallant man; I told him that I would
very fain buy a horse, and if it were possible, the
horse I saw but a little before; but he telling me
none was to be sold there, I offered to leave in his
hands one hundred pieces, if he would lend me a good

horse for a day or two, he to restore me the money again when I delivered him the horse in good plight, and did besides bring him some present as a gratuity.

The lieutenant, though he did not know me, suspected I had some private quarrel, and that I desired this horse to fight on, and thereupon told me, " Sir, whosoever you are, you seem to be a person of worth, and you shall have the best horse in the stable ; and if you have a quarrel and want a second, I offer myself to serve you upon another horse, and if you will let me go along with you upon these terms, I will ask no pawn of you for the horse." I told him I would use no second, and I desired him to accept one hundred pieces, which I had there about me, in pawn for the horse, and he should hear from me shortly again ; and that though I did not take his noble offer of coming along with me, I should evermore rest much obliged to him ; whereupon giving him my purse with the money in it, I got upon his horse, and left my nag besides with him.

Riding thus away about twelve o'clock at night to the wood from whence I came, I alighted from my horse and rested there till morning ; the day now breaking I got on horseback, and attended the Lord of Walden and his second. The first person that appeared was a footman, who I heard afterwards was sent by the Lady of Walden, who as soon as he saw me, ran back again with all speed ; I meant once to pursue him, but that I thought it better at last to keep my place. About two hours after Sir William St. Leger, now Lord President of

Munster, came to me, and told me he knew the cause of my being there, and that the business was discovered by the Lord Walden's rising so early that morning, and the suspicion that he meant to fight with me, and had Sir Thomas Peyton with him, and that he would ride to him, and that there were thirty or forty sent after us, to hinder us from meeting ; shortly after many more came to the place where I was, and told me I must not fight, and that they were sent for the same purpose, and that it was to no purpose to stay there, and thence rode to seek the Lord of Walden ; I stayed yet two hours longer, but finding still more company came in, rode back again to the Scotch quarters, and delivered the horse back again, and received my money and nag from Lieutenant Montgomery, and so withdrew myself to the French quarters, till I did find some convenient time to send again to the Lord Walden.

Being among the French, I remembered myself of the bravado of Monsieur Balagny, and coming to him told him, I knew how brave a man he was, and that as he had put me to one trial of daring, when I was last with him in his trenches, I would put him to another ; saying, I heard he had a fair mistress, and that the scarf he wore was her gift, and that I would maintain I had a worthier mistress than he, and that I would do as much for her sake as he, or any else durst do for his. Balagny hereupon looking merrily upon me, said, "If we shall try who is the abler man to serve his mistress, let both of us get two wenches, and he that doth his business best, let him be the braver man; and that for his part, he had no mind to fight on that quarrel." I looking hereupon somewhat disdainfully on him, said he spoke more like a paillard[1] than a cavalier; to which he answering nothing, I rode my ways, and afterwards went to Monsieur Terant, a French gentleman that belonged to the Duke of Montmorency, formerly mentioned; who telling me he had a quarrel with another gentleman, I offered to be his second, but he saying he was provided already, I rode thence to the English quarters, attending some fit occasion to send again to the Lord Walden. I came no sooner thither, but I found Sir Thomas Somerset[2] with eleven or twelve more in the head of the English, who were then drawing forth in a body or squadron, who seeing me on horseback, with a footman only that attended me, gave me some affronting words, for my quarrelling with the Lord of Walden; whereupon I alighted, and giving my horse to my lackey, drew my sword, which he no sooner saw but he drew his, as also all the company with him. I running hereupon amongst them, put by some of their thrusts, and making towards him in particular, put by a thrust of his, and had certainly run him through, but that one Lieutenant Prichard, at that instant taking me by the shoulder, turned me aside; but I recovering myself again, ran at him a second time,

---

[1] A loose fellow.

[2] He was third son of Edward, Earl of Worcester, Lord Privy Seal to Queen Elizabeth and King James. Sir Thomas Somerset was Master of the Horse to Queen Anne, was made Knight of the Bath in 1604, and, later, Viscount Somerset, of Cashel, in Ireland.

which he perceiving, retired himself with the company to the tents which were near, though not so fast but I hurt one Proger, and some others also that were with him. But they being all at last got within the tents, I finding now nothing else to be done, got to my horse again, having received only a slight hurt on the outside of my ribs, and two thrusts, the one through the skirts of my doublet, and the other through my breeches, and about eighteen nicks upon my sword and hilt, and so rode to the trenches before Juliers, where our soldiers were.

Not long after this, the town being now sur- rendered, and every body preparing to go their ways, I sent again a gentleman to the Lord of Walden to offer him the meeting with my sword, but this was avoided not very handsomely by him (contrary to what Sir Henry Rich, now Earl of Holland, persuaded him).

After having taken leave of his excellency Sir Edward Cecil, I thought fit to return on my way homewards as far as Dusseldorf. I had been scarce two hours in my lodgings when one Lieutenant Hamilton brought a letter from Sir James Areskin (who was then in town likewise) unto me, the effect whereof was, that in regard his Lieutenant Mont- gomery had told him that I had the said James Areskin's consent for borrowing his horse, he did desire me to do one of two things, which was, either to disavow the said words, which he thought in his conscience I never spake ; or, if I would justify them then to appoint time and place to fight with him.

Having considered a while what I was to do in this case, I told Lieutenant Hamilton that I thought myself bound in honour to accept the more noble part of his proposition, which was to fight with him, when yet perchance it might be easy enough for me to say that I had his horse upon other terms than was affirmed; whereupon also giving Lieutenant Hamilton the length of my sword, I told him that as soon as ever he had matched it, I would fight with him, wishing him further to make haste, since I desired to end the business as speedily as could be. Lieutenant Hamilton hereupon returning back, met in a cross street (I know not by what miraculous adventure) Lieutenant Montgomery, conveying divers of the hurt and maimed soldiers at the siege of Juliers unto that town, to be lodged and dressed by the surgeons there; Hamilton hereupon calling to Montgomery, told him the effects of his captain's letter, together with my answer, which Montgomery no sooner heard, but he replied (as Hamilton told me afterwards), "I see that noble gentleman chooseth rather to fight than to contradict me; but my telling a lie must not be an occasion why either my captain or he should hazard their lives: I will alight from my horse, and tell my captain presently how all that matter past;" whereupon also he relating the business about borrowing the horse, in that manner I formerly set down, which as soon as Sir James Areskin heard, he sent Lieutenant Hamilton to me presently again, to tell me he was satisfied how the business past, and that he had nothing to say to me, but that he was my most humble servant, and was sorry he had ever questioned me in that manner.

Some occasions detaining me in Dusseldorf, the next day Lieutenant Montgomery came to me, and told me he was in danger of losing his place, and desired me to make means to his excellency the Prince of Orange that he might not be cashiered, or else that he was undone. I told him that either I would keep him in his place, or take him as my companion and friend, and allow him sufficient means till I could provide him another as good as it; which he taking very kindly, but desiring chiefly he might go with my letter to the Prince of Orange, I obtained at last he should be restored to his place again.

And now taking boat, I passed along the river of Rhine to the Low Countries, where after some stay, I went to Antwerp and Brussels; and having passed some time in the court there, went from thence to Calais, where taking ship, I arrived at Dover, and so went to London. I had scarce been two days there, when the lords of the council sending for me, ended the difference betwixt the Lord of Walden and myself. And, now if I may say it without vanity, I was in great esteem both in court and city; many of the greatest desiring my company, though yet before that time I had no acquaintance with them. Richard,[1] Earl of Dorset, to whom otherwise I was a stranger, one day invited me to Dorset House, where bringing me

---

[1] Richard Sackville, Earl of Dorset, grandson of the Treasurer, and husband of the famous Anne Clifford, Countess of Dorset and Pembroke.

into his gallery, and showing me many pictures, he at last brought me to a frame covered with green taffeta, and asked me who I thought was there; and therewithal presently drawing the curtain, showed me my own picture; whereupon demanding how his lordship came to have it, he answered, that he had heard so many brave things of me, that he got a copy of a picture which one Larkin[1] a painter drew for me, the original whereof I intended before my departure to the Low Countries for Sir Thomas Lucy. But not only the Earl of Dorset, but a greater person[2] than I will here nominate, got another copy from Larkin, and placing it afterwards in her cabinet (without that ever I knew any such thing was done), gave occasion to those who saw it after her death of more discourse than I could have wished; and indeed I may truly say, that taking of my picture was fatal to me, for more reasons than I shall think fit to deliver.

There was a lady also, wife to Sir John Ayres, knight, who finding some means to get a copy of my picture from Larkin, gave it to Mr. Isaac Oliver,[3] the painter in Blackfriars, and desired him to draw it in little after his manner ; which being done, she caused it to be set in gold and enamelled, and so wore it about her neck, so low that she hid it under her breasts, which, I conceive, coming afterwards to the

---

[1] M. de Rémusat was unable to identify Larkin, and Mr. Lee supposes Nicholas *Lockie* to be meant.

[2] This was probably Queen Anne, as appears from the terms in which he speaks of her a little farther.

[3] A famous miniature-painter of the time. —*Lee.*

knowledge of Sir John Ayres, gave him more cause of
jealousy than needed, had he known how innocent I
was from pretending to any thing which might wrong
him or his lady; since I could not so much as imagine
that either she had my picture, or that she bare more
than ordinary affection to me. It is true that she had
a place in court, and attended Queen Anne, and was
beside of an excellent wit and discourse, she had made
herself a considerable person; howbeit little more
than common civility ever passed betwixt us, though
I confess I think no man was welcomer to her when
I came, for which I shall allege this passage :—

Coming one day into her chamber, I saw her
through the curtains lying upon her bed with a wax
candle in one hand, and the picture I formerly mentioned in the other. I coming thereupon somewhat
boldly to her, she blew out the candle, and hid the
picture from me; myself thereupon being curious to
know what that was she held in her hand, got the
candle to be lighted again, by means whereof I found
it was my picture she looked upon with more earnestness and passion than I could have easily believed,
especially since myself was not engaged in any affection
towards her. I could willingly have omitted this
passage, but that it was the beginning of a bloody
history which followed: howsoever, yet I must before
the Eternal God clear her honour.

And now in court a great person[1] sent for me
divers times to attend her, which summons though I

---

[1] Another allusion to Queen Anne.

obeyed, yet God knoweth I declined coming to her as much as conveniently I could, without incurring her displeasure; and this I did not only for very honest reasons, but, to speak ingenuously, because that affection passed betwixt me and another lady [1] (who I believe was the fairest of her time) as nothing could divert it. I had not been long in London, when a violent burning fever seized upon me, which brought me almost to my death, though at last I did by slow degrees recover my health.

Being thus upon my amendment, the Lord Lisle,[2] afterwards Earl of Leicester, sent me word that Sir John Ayres intended to kill me in my bed, and wished me keep a guard upon my chamber and person. The same advertisement was confirmed by Lucy,[3] Countess of Bedford, and the Lady Hobby [4] shortly after. Hereupon I thought fit to entreat Sir William Herbert, now Lord Powis, to go to Sir John Ayres, and tell him that I marvelled much at the information given me by these great persons, and that I could not imagine any sufficient ground hereof; howbeit, if he had any thing to say to me in a fair and noble way, I would give him the meeting as soon as I had got strength enough to stand upon my legs. Sir William hereupon brought me so ambiguous and doubtful an

---

[1] Probably Lady Kent.

[2] Robert Sidney, younger brother of Sir Philip Sidney.

[3] Lucy Harrington, wife of Edward, Earl of Bedford, patroness of the wits and poets of her day.

[4] Probably Anne, second wife of Sir Edward Hobby, a patron of Camden.

answer from him, that whatsoever he meant, he would not declare yet his intention, which was really, as I found afterwards, to kill me any way that he could, since, as he said, though falsely, I had whored his wife. Finding no means thus to surprise me, he sent me a letter to this effect; that he desired to meet me somewhere, and that it might so fall out as I might return quietly again. To· this I replied, that if he desired to fight with me upon equal terms, I should upon assurance of the field and fair play, give him meeting when he did any way specify the cause, and that I did not think fit to come to him upon any other terms, having been sufficiently informed of his plots to assassinate me.

After this, finding he could take no advantage against me, then, in a treacherous way, he resolved to assassinate me in this manner; hearing I was to come to Whitehall on horseback, with two lackeys only, he attended my coming back in a place called Scotland Yard, at the hither end of Whitehall, as you come to it from the Strand, hiding himself here with four men armed, on purpose to kill me.

I took horse at Whitehall Gate, and passing by that place, he being armed with a sword and dagger, without giving me so much as the least warning, ran at me furiously, but instead of me, wounded my horse in the brisket, as far as his sword could enter for the bone. My horse hereupon starting aside, he ran him again in the shoulder, which, though it made the horse more timorous, yet gave me time to draw my sword. His men thereupon encompassed me, and wounded my horse in three places more ; this made my horse kick and fling in that manner, as his men durst not come near me ; which advantage I took to strike at Sir John Ayres with all my force, but he warded the blow both with his sword and dagger ; instead of doing him harm, I broke my sword within a foot of the hilt. Hereupon some passenger that knew me, and observing my horse bleeding in so many places, and so many men assaulting me, and my sword broken, cried to me several times, " Ride away, ride away ;" but I, scorning a base flight upon what terms soever, instead thereof, alighted as well as I could from my horse.

I had no sooner put one foot upon the ground, but Sir John Ayres pursuing me, made at my horse again, which the horse perceiving, pressed on me on the side I alighted, in that manner that he threw me down, so that I remained flat upon the ground, only one foot hanging in the stirrup, with that piece of a sword in my right hand. Sir John Ayres hereupon ran about the horse, and was thrusting his sword into me, when I, finding myself in this danger, did with both my arms reaching at his legs, pull them towards me, till he fell down backwards on his head. One of my footmen hereupon, who was a little Shropshire boy, freed my foot out of the stirrup ; the other, which was a great fellow, having run away as soon as he saw the first assault. This gave me time to get upon my legs, and to put myself in the best posture I could with that poor remnant of a weapon.

Sir John Ayres by this time likewise was got up, standing betwixt me and some part of Whitehall, with

two men on each side of him, and his brother behind
him, with at least twenty or thirty persons of his
friends, or attendants of the Earl of Suffolk.[1] Observing thus a body of men standing in opposition
against me, though to speak truly I saw no swords
drawn, but by Sir John Ayres and his men, I ran
violently against Sir John Ayres; but he knowing
my sword had no point, held his sword and dagger
over his head, as believing I could strike rather than
thrust; which I no sooner perceived but I put a
home thrust to the middle of his breast, that I
threw him down with so much force, that his head
fell first to the ground, and his heel upwards. His
men hereupon assaulted me; when one, Mr. Mansel, a
Glamorganshire gentleman, finding so many set against
me alone, closed with one of them; a Scotch gentleman also closing with another, took him off also. All
I could well do to those two which remained was, to
ward their thrusts, which I did with that resolution,
that I got ground upon them.

Sir John Ayres was now got up a third time, when
I was making towards him with the intention to close,
thinking that there was otherwise no safety for me,
put by a thrust of his with my left hand, and so
coming within him, received a stab with his dagger
on my right side, which ran down my ribs as far as
my hip, which I feeling, did with my right elbow
force his hand, together with the hilt of the dagger,

---

[1] Father of Lord Howard of Walden, with whom Herbert had lately
quarrelled.—*Lee.*

so near the upper part of my right side, that I made him leave hold. The dagger now sticking in me, Sir Henry Cary, afterwards Lord of Falkland, and Lord Deputy of Ireland, finding the dagger thus in my body, snatched it out. This while I being closed with Sir John Ayres, hurt him on the head, and threw him down a third time, when, kneeling on the ground, and bestriding him, I struck at him as hard as I could with my piece of a sword, and wounded him in four several places, and did almost cut off his left hand. His two men this while struck at me; but it pleased God even miraculously to defend me; for when I lifted up my sword to strike at Sir John Ayres, I bore off their blows half a dozen times. His friends now finding him in this danger, took him by the head and shoulders, and drew him from betwixt my legs, and carried him along with them through Whitehall, at the stairs whereof he took boat. Sir Herbert Croft (as he told me afterwards) met him upon the water, vomiting all the way, which I believe was caused by the violence of the first thrust I gave him. His servants, brother, and friends being now retired also, I remained master of the place and his weapons; having first wrested his dagger from him, and afterwards struck his sword out of his hand.

This being done, I retired to a friend's house in the Strand, where I sent for a surgeon, who, searching my wound on the right side, and finding it not to be mortal, cured me in the space of some ten days, during which time I received many noble visits and messages from some of the best in the kingdom.

Being now fully recovered of my hurts, I desired Sir Robert Harley[1] to go to Sir John Ayres, and tell him, that though I thought he had not so much honour left in him that I could be any way ambitious to get it, yet that I desired to see him in the field with his sword in his hand. The answer that he sent me was, that I had whored his wife, and that he would kill me with a musket out of a window.

The Lords of the Privy Council, who had first sent for my sword, that they might see the little fragment of a weapon with which I had so behaved myself, as perchance the like had not been heard in any credible way, did afterwards command both him and me to appear before them; but I absenting myself on purpose, sent one Humphrey Hill with a challenge to him in an ordinary, which he refusing to receive, Humphrey Hill put it upon the point of his sword, and so let it fall before him and the company then present.

The Lords of the Privy Council had now taken order to apprehend Sir John Ayres, when I, finding nothing else to be done, submitted myself likewise to them. Sir John Ayres had now published everywhere, that the ground of his jealousy, and consequently of his assaulting me, was drawn from the confession of his wife the Lady Ayres. She, to vindicate her honour, as well as free me from this accusation, sent a letter to her aunt the Lady Crook, to this purpose; that her husband Sir John Ayres did lie falsely, in saying that I ever whored her; but most falsely of all did lie,

---

[1] Knight of the Bath, and Master of the Mint.

when he said he had it from her confession, for she had never said any such thing.

This letter the Lady Crook presented to me most opportunely, as I was going to the Council table before the Lords, who having examined Sir John Ayres concerning the cause of the quarrel against me, found him still persist in his wife's confession of the fact; and now he being withdrawn, I was sent for, when the Duke of Lennox,[1] afterwards of Richmond, telling me that was the ground of his quarrel, and the only excuse he had for assaulting me in that manner, I desired his lordship to peruse the letter, which I told him was given me as I came into the room. This letter being publicly read by a clerk of the Council, the Duke of Lennox then said, that he thought Sir John Ayres the most miserable man living; for his wife had not only given him the lie, as he found by her letter, but his father had disinherited him for attempting to kill me in that barbarous fashion, which was most true, as I found afterwards. For the rest, that I might content myself with what I had done, it being more almost than could be believed, but that I had so many witnesses thereof; for all which reasons he commanded me, in the name of his Majesty, and all their Lordships, not to send any more to Sir John Ayres, nor to receive any message from him, in the way of fighting; which commandment I observed. Howbeit, I must not omit to tell, that some years

---

[1] Lodovic Stuart, Duke of Lennox and Richmond, was Lord Steward of the Household, and Knight of the Garter.

afterwards, Sir John Ayres returning from Ireland by Beaumaris, where I then was, some of my servants and followers broke open the doors of the house where he was, and would (I believe) have cut him into pieces, but that I, hearing thereof, came suddenly to the house and recalled them, sending him word also, that I scorned to give him the usage he gave me, and that I would set him free out of the town; which courtesy of mine, as I was told afterwards, he did thankfully acknowledge.

About a month after that Sir John Ayres attempted to assassinate me, the news thereof was carried, I know not how, to the Duke of Montmorency, who presently dispatched a gentleman with a letter to me (which I keep), and a kind offer, that if I would come unto him, I should be used as his own son; neither had this gentleman, as I know of, any other business in England. I was told besides by this gentleman, that the Duke heard I had greater and more powerful enemies than did publicly declare themselves (which, indeed, was true), and that he doubted I might have a mischief before I was aware.

My answer hereunto by letter was, That I rendered most humble thanks for his great favour in sending to me; that no enemies, how great or many soever, could force me out of the kingdom; but if ever there were occasion to serve him in particular, I should not fail to come; for performance whereof, it happening there were some overtures of a civil war in France the next year, I sent over a French gentleman who attended me, unto the Duke of Montmorency, expressly to tell him, that if he had occasion to use my service in the designed war, I would bring over one hundred horse at my own cost and charges to him ; which that good old Duke and constable took so kindly, that, as the Duchess of Ventadour, his daughter, told me afterwards, when I was ambassador, there were few days, till the last of his life, that he did not speak of me with much affection.

I can say little more memorable concerning myself from the year 1611, when I was hurt, until the year of our Lord 1614, than that I passed my time sometimes in the Court, where (I protest before God) I had more favours than I desired ; and sometimes in the country, without any memorable accident ; but only that it happened one time, going from St. Julian's to Abergavenny, in the way to Montgomery Castle, Richard Griffiths, a servant of mine, being come near a bridge over Usk, not far from the town, thought fit to water his horse ; but the river being deep and strong in that place where he entered it, he was carried down the stream. My servants that were before me, seeing this, cried aloud, "Dick Griffiths was drowning :" which I no sooner heard, but I put my spurs to my horse, and coming up to the place, where I saw him as high as his middle in water, leapt into the river a little below him, and swimming up to him, bore him up with one of my hands, and brought him unto the middle of the river, where (through God's great providence) was a bank of sand. Coming hither not without some difficulty, we rested ourselves ; and advised whether it were better to return back unto the side from whence we came, or to go on forwards; but Dick Griffiths saying we were sure to swim if we returned back, and that, perchance, the river might be shallow the other way, I followed his counsel, and putting my horse below him, bore him up in the manner I did formerly, and swimming through the river, brought him safe to the other side. The horse I rode upon, I remember, cost me forty pounds, and was the same horse which Sir John Ayres hurt under me, and did swim excellently well, carrying me and his back above water; whereas that little nag upon which Richard Griffiths rid, swam so low, that he must needs have drowned, if I had not supported him.

I will tell one history more of this horse, which I bought of my cousin Fowler of the Grange, because it is memorable. I was passing over a bridge not far from Colebrook, which had no barrier on the one side, and a hole in the bridge, not far from the middle; my horse, though lusty, yet being very timorous, and seeing besides but very little on the right eye, started so much at the hole, that upon a sudden he had put half his body lengthwise over the side of the bridge, and was ready to fall into the river, with his fore-foot and hinder-foot on the right side; when I, foreseeing the danger I was in if I fell down, clapt my left foot, together with the stirrup and spur, flat-long to the left side, and so made him leap upon all four into the river, whence, after some three or four plunges, he brought me to land.

The year 1614 was now entering, when I understood

that the Low Country and Spanish army would be in the field that year. This made me resolve to offer my service to the Prince of Orange, who, upon my coming, did much welcome me, not suffering me almost to eat anywhere but at his table, and carrying me abroad the afternoon in his coach, to partake of those entertainments he delighted in when there was no pressing occasion. The Low Country army being now ready, his Excellency prepared to go into the field ; in the way to which, he took me in his coach, and sometimes in a waggon, after the Low Country fashion, to the great envy of the English and French chief commanders, who expected that honour.

Being now arrived near Emmerich, one with a most humble petition came from a monastery of nuns, most humbly desiring that the soldiers might not violate their honour, nor their monastery ; whereupon, I was a most humble suitor to his Excellency to spare them, which he granted ; " But," said he, " we will go and see them ourselves ; " and thus, his Excellency, and I and Sir Charles Morgan only, not long after going to the monastery, found it deserted in great part. Having put a guard upon this monastery, his Excellency marched with his army on till we came near the city of Emmerich, which, upon summoning, yielded ; and now leaving a garrison here, we resolved to march towards Rees.

This place, having the Spanish army, under the command of Monsieur Spinola, on the one side, and the Low Country army on the other, being able to resist neither, sent word to both armies, that whichsoever came first should have the place. Spinola hereupon sent word to his Excellency, that if we intended to take Rees, he would give him battle in a plain near before the town. His Excellency, nothing astonished hereat, marched on, his pioneers making his way for the army still, through hedges and ditches, until he came to that hedge and ditch which was next the plain; and here drawing his men into battle, resolved to attend the coming of Spinola into the field. While his men were putting in order, I was so desirous to see whether Spinola with his army appeared, I leapt over a great hedge and ditch, attended only with one footman, purposing to change a pistol-shot or two with the first I met. I found thus some single horse in the field, who, perceiving me to come on, rid away as fast as they could, believing, perchance, that more would follow me. Having thus passed to the further end of the field, and finding no show of the enemy, I returned back, that I might inform his Excellency there was no hope of fighting, as I could perceive. In the mean time, his Excellency having prepared all things for battle, sent out five or six scouts to discover whether the enemy were coming, according to promise; these men finding me now coming towards them, thought I was one of the enemies, which being perceived by me, and I as little knowing at that time who they were, rode up with my sword in my hand and pistol, to encounter them; and now being come within reasonable distance, one of the persons there that knew me, told his fellows who I was, whereupon I passed quietly to his Excellency, and told him what

I had done, and that I found no appearance of an army. His Excellency then caused the hedge and ditch before him to be levelled, and marched in front, with his army, into the middle of the field; from whence, sending some of his forces to summon the town, it yielded without resistance.

Our army made that haste to come to the place appointed for the battle, that all our baggage and provision were left behind, insomuch that I was without any meat, but what my footman spared me out of his pocket; and my lodging that night was no better, for extreme rain falling at that time in the open field, I had no shelter, but was glad to get on the top of a waggon which had straw in it, and to cover myself with my cloak as well as I could, and so endure that stormy night. Morning being come, and no enemy appearing, I went to the town of Rees, into which his Excellency having now put a garrison, marched on with the rest of his army towards Wezel, before which Spinola with his army lay, and in the way intrenched himself strongly, and attended Spinola's motions. For the rest, nothing memorable happened after this betwixt those two generals, for the space of many weeks.

I must yet not omit with thankfulness to remember a favour his Excellency did me at this time; for a soldier having killed his fellow soldier in the quarter where they were lodged, which is an unpardonable fault, insomuch that no man would speak for him; the poor fellow comes to me, and desires me to beg his life of his Excellency; whereupon I demanding whether he had ever heard of a man pardoned in this kind, and he saying no, I told him it was in vain then for me to speak ; when the poor fellow writhing his neck a little, said, " Sir, but were it not better you shall cast away a few words, than I lose my life ? " This piece of eloquence moved me so much, that I went strait to his Excellency, and told him what the poor fellow had said, desiring him to excuse me, if upon these terms I took the boldness to speak for him. There was present at that time the Earl of Southampton,[1] as also Sir Edward Cecil, and Sir Horace Vere, as also Monsieur de Châtillon, and divers other French commanders ; to whom his Excellency turning himself said in French, " Do you see this cavalier with all that courage you know, hath yet that good-nature to pray for the life of a poor soldier ? though I have never pardoned any before in this kind, yet I will pardon this at his request ; " so commanding him to be brought me, and disposed of as I thought fit, whom therefore I released and set free.

It was now so far advanced in autumn, both armies thought of retiring themselves into their garrisons, when a trumpeter comes from the Spanish army to ours, with a challenge from a Spanish cavalier to this effect, That if any cavalier in our army would fight a single combat for the sake of his mistress, the said Spaniard would meet him, upon assurance of the camp in our army. This challenge being brought

---

[1] Henry Wriothesley, third Earl of Southampton. He had been attainted with the Earl of Essex, but was restored by King James, and made Knight of the Garter.

early in the morning was accepted by nobody till about ten or eleven of the clock, when a report thereof coming to me, I went strait to his Excellency, and told him I desired to accept the challenge. His Excellency thereupon looking earnestly upon me, told me he was an old soldier, and that he had observed two sorts of men who used to send challenges in this kind; one was of those who having lost perchance some part of their honour in the field against the enemy, would recover it again by a single fight. The other was of those who sent it only to discover whether our army had in it men affected to give trial of themselves in this kind; howbeit, if this man was a person without exception to be taken against him, he said there was none he knew, upon whom he would sooner venture the honour of his army than myself; and this also he spoke before divers of the English and French commanders I formerly nominated.

Hereupon, by his Excellency's permission, I sent a trumpet to the Spanish army with this answer, " That if the person who would be sent were a cavalier without reproach, I would answer him with such weapons as we should agree upon, in the place he offered ;" but my trumpeter was scarcely arrived, as I believe, at the Spanish army, when another trumpeter came to ours from Spinola, saying the challenge was made without his consent, and that therefore he would not permit it.

This message being brought to his Excellency, with whom I then was, he said to me presently, " This is strange; they send a challenge hither, and when they have done, recall it : I should be glad if I knew the true causes of it."—" Sir," said I, "if you will give me leave, I will go to their army and make the like challenge as they sent hither ; it may be some scruple is made concerning the place appointed, being in your Excellency's camp, and therefore I shall offer them the combat in their own ;" his Excellency said, "I should never have persuaded you to this course, but since you voluntarily offer it, I must not deny that which you think to be for your honour."

Hereupon taking my leave of him, and desiring Sir Humphrey Tufton,[1] a brave gentleman, to bear me company, thus we two, attended only with two lackeys, rode straight towards the Spanish camp before Wezel; coming thither without any disturbance, by the way I was demanded by the guard at the entering into the camp, with whom I would speak ; I told them with the Duke of Neuburg ; whereupon a soldier was presently sent with us to conduct us to the Duke of Neuburg's tent, who remembering me well, since he saw me at the siege of Juliers, very kindly embraced me, and therewithal demanding the cause of my coming thither ; I told him the effect thereof in the manner I formerly set down ; to which he replied only, he would acquaint the Marquis Spinola therewith ; who coming shortly after to the Duke of Neuburg's tent, with a great train of commanders and captains following him, he no sooner

---

[1] Third son of Sir John Tufton, and brother of Nicholas Earl of Thanet.

entered but he turned to me and said, that he knew
well the cause of my coming, and that the same reasons
which made him forbid the Spanish cavalier to fight
a combat in the Prince of Orange's camp, did make
him forbid it in his, and that no one should be
better welcome to him than I would be, and thereupon
entreated me to come and dine with him; I finding
nothing else to be done, did kindly accept the offer;
and so attending him to his tent, where a brave
dinner being put upon his table, he placed the Duke
of Neuburg uppermost at one end of the table, and
myself at the other, himself sitting below us, presenting with his own hand still the best of that meat his
carver offered him. He demanded of me then in Italian,
" *Di che moriva Sigr. Francisco Vere*" (Of what died
Sir Francis Vere?) I told him, " *Per aver niente à
fare*" (Because he had nothing to do.) Spinola replied,
" *E basta per un generale*" (And it is enough to kill a
general). And indeed that brave commander, Sir
Francis Vere, died not in the time of war but of peace.

Taking my leave now of the Marquis Spinola, I
told him that if ever he did lead an army against the
Infidels, I should adventure to be the first man that
would die in that quarrel, and together demanded
leave of him to see his army, which he granting, I
took leave of him, and did at leisure view it;
observing the difference in the proceedings betwixt
the Low Country army and fortifications, as well as
I could; and so returning shortly after to his
Excellency, related to him the success of my journey.

It happened about this time that Sir Henry

Wotton mediated a peace, by the king's command, who coming for that purpose to Wezel, I took occasion to go along with him to Spinola's army, . whence after a night's stay, I went on an extreme rainy day through the woods to Kaiserswerth, to the great wonder of mine host, who said all men were robbed or killed that went that way; from hence I went to Cologne, where among other things I saw the monastery of St. Herbert; from hence I went to Heidelberg, where I saw the Prince and Princess Palatine, from whom having received much good usage, I went to Ulm, and so to Ausburg, where extraordinary honour was done me; for coming into an inn, where an ambassador from Brussels lay, the town sent twenty great flagons of wine thither, whereof they gave eleven to the ambassador, and nine to me; and withal some such compliments that I found my fame had prevented[1] my coming thither.

From hence I went through Switzerland to Trent, and from thence to Venice, where I was received by the English ambassador, Sir Dudley Carlton,[2] with much honour. Among other favours shewed me, I was brought to see a nun in Murano, who being an admired beauty, and together singing extremely well, was thought one of the rarities not only of that place but of the time. We came to a room opposite unto the cloister, whence she coming on the other side of the grate betwixt us, sung so extremely well, that

---

[1] *i.e.,* preceded.

[2] Ambassador to Venice, Savoy, and Holland, Secretary of State, and Viscount Dorchester.

when she departed neither my Lord Ambassador nor his lady, who were then present, could find as much as a word of fitting language to return her, for the extraordinary music she gave us; when I, being ashamed that she should go back without some testimony of the sense we had both of the harmony of her beauty and her voice, said in Italian, "*Moria pur quando vuol, non bisogna mutar ni voce ni facia per esser un angelo*" ("Die whensoever you will, you neither need to change voice nor face to be an angel"). These words it seemed were fatal, for going thence to Rome, and returning shortly afterwards, I heard she was dead in the meantime.

From Venice, after some stay, I went to Florence, where I met the Earl of Oxford[1] and Sir Benjamin Rudyerd ;[2] having seen the rarities of this place likewise, and particularly that rare chapel made for the house of Medici, beautified on all the inside with a coarser kind of precious stone, as also that nail which was at one end iron, and the other gold, made so by virtue of a tincture into which it was put. I went to Siena, and from thence, a little before the Christmas holidays, to Rome. 1 was no sooner alighted at my inn, but I went straight to the English College, where demanding for the regent or master thereof, a grave person not long after appeared at the door, to whom

---

[1] Henry Vere, Earl of Oxford.   He died at the Hague in 1625, of a sickness contracted at the siege of Breda.

[2] Sir Benjamin Rudyerd, a wit and poet, and intimate friend of William Earl of Pembroke, with whose poems Sir Benjamin's are printed.

I spake in this manner: "Sir, I need not tell you my country when you hear my language; I come not here to study controversies, but to see the antiquities of the place; if without scandal to the religion in which I was born and bred up, I may take this liberty, I should be glad to spend some convenient time here; if not, my horse is yet unsaddled, and myself willing to go out of town." The answer returned by him to me was, that he never heard anybody before me profess himself of any other religion than what was used in Rome; for his part, he approved much my freedom, as collecting thereby I was a person of honour; for the rest, that he could give me no warrant for my stay there, howbeit that experience did teach that those men who gave no affronts to the Roman Catholic religion, received none; whereupon also he demanded my name. I telling him I was called Sir Edward Herbert, he replied, that he had heard men oftentimes speak of me both for learning and courage, and presently invited me to dinner; I told him that "I took his courteous offer as an argument of his affection; that I desired him to excuse me, if I did not accept it; the uttermost liberty I had (as the times then were in England) being already taken in coming to that city only, least they should think me a factious person; I thought fit to tell him that I conceived the points agreed upon on both sides, are greater bonds of amity betwixt us, than that the points disagreed on could break them; that for my part I loved everybody that was of a pious and virtuous life, and thought the errors on

what side soever, were more worthy pity than hate ; "
and having declared myself thus far, I took my leave
of him courteously and spent about a month's time in
seeing the antiquities of that place which first found
means to establish so great an empire over the persons
of men, and afterwards over their consciences ; the
articles of confession and absolving sinners, being a
greater *arcanum imperii* for governing the world
than all the arts invented by statists formerly were.

After I had seen Rome sufficiently, I went to
Tivoli, anciently called Tibur, and saw the fair palace
and garden there, as also Frascati, anciently called
Tusculanum. After that I returned to Rome, and
saw the Pope in consistory, which being done, when
the Pope being now ready to give his blessing, I
departed thence suddenly, which gave such a suspicion of me, that some were sent to apprehend
me, but I going a byway escaped them, and went to
my inn to take horse, where I had not been now half
an hour, when the master or regent of the English
College telling me that I was accused in the Inquisition, and that I could stay no longer with any safety,
I took this warning very kindly ; howbeit I did only
for the present change my lodging, and a day or two
afterwards took horse and went out of Rome towards
Siena, and from thence to Florence.

I saw Robert Dudley,[1] who had the title of Earl or

---

[1] See account in Catalogue of Royal and Noble Authors, vol. ii.
Handsome Mrs. Sudel was Mrs. Southwell, daughter of Sir Robert
Southwell, who had followed Sir Robert Dudley from England, under
the disguise of a page.

Duke of Northumberland given him by the Emperor,[1] and handsome Mrs. Southwell, whom he carried with him out of England, and was there taken for his wife. I was invited by them to a great feast the night before I went out of town; taking my leave of them both, I prepared for my journey the next morning; when I was ready to depart, a messenger came to me, and told me if I would accept the same pension Sir Robert Dudley had, being two thousand ducats per annum, the duke would entertain me for his service in the war against the Turks. This offer, whether procured by the means of Sir Robert Dudley, Mrs. Southwell, or Sigr. Loty, my ancient friend, I know not, being thankfully acknowledged as a great honour, was yet refused by me, my intention being to serve his Excellency in the Low Country war.

After I had stayed a while, from hence I went by Ferrara and Bologna towards Padua, in which university having spent some time to hear the learned readers, and particularly Cremonini,[2] I left my English horses and Scotch saddles there, for on them I rid all the way from the Low Countries, I went by boat to Venice. The Lord Ambassador, Sir Dudley Carlton, by this time had a command to reside a while in the court of the Duke of Savoy, wherewith also his Lordship acquainted me, demanding whether I would go thither; this offer was gladly accepted by

---

[1] Ferdinand I.

[2] 1552 1631 Professor of Philosophy at Padua. The last important representative of Aristotelianism as tempered by Averroës.

me, both as I was desirous to see that court, and that it was in the way to the Low Country, where I meant to see the war in the summer ensuing.

Coming thus in the coach with my Lord Ambassador to Milan, the governor thereof invited my Lord Ambassador to his house, and sometimes feasted him during his stay there. Here I heard that famous nun singing to the organ in this manner; another nun beginning first to sing, performed her part so well, that we gave her much applause for her excellent art and voice; only we thought she did sing somewhat lower than other women usually did; hereupon also, being ready to depart, we heard suddenly, for we saw nobody, that nun which was so famous, sing an eight higher than the other had done. Her voice was the sweetest, strongest, and clearest, that ever I heard; in the using whereof, also, she shewed that art as ravished us into admiration.

From Milan we went to Novara, as I remember, where we were entertained by the governor, being a Spaniard, with one of the most sumptuous feasts that ever I saw, being but of nine dishes, in three several services; the first whereof was, three ollas podridas, consisting of all choice boiled meats, placed in three large silver chargers, which took up the length of a great table; the meat in it being heightened up artificially pyramid-wise, to a sparrow which was on the top; the second service was like the former, of roast meat, in which all manner of fowl, from the pheasant and partridge, to other fowl less than them, were heightened up to a lark; the third was in sweetmeats, dry of all sorts, heightened in like manner to a round comfit.

From hence we went to Vercelli, a town of the Duke of Savoy's, frontier to the Spaniard, with whom the Duke was then in war; from whence, passing by places of least note, we came to Turin, where the Duke of Savoy's court was. After I had refreshed myself here some two or three days, I took leave of my Lord Ambassador, with intention to go to the Low Countries, and was now upon the way thither, as far as the foot of Mount Cenis, when the Count Scarnafissi came to me from the Duke,[1] and brought a letter to this effect: "That the Duke had heard I was a cavalier of great worth, and desirous to see the wars, and that if I would serve him, I should make my own conditions." Finding so courteous an invitation, I returned back, and was lodged by the Duke of Savoy in a chamber furnished with silk and gold hangings, and a very rich bed, and defrayed at the Duke's charges, in the English ambassador's house. The Duke also confirmed unto me what the Count Scarnafissi had said, and together bestowed divers compliments on me. I told his Highness, that when I knew in what service he pleased to employ me, he should find me ready to testify the sense I had of his princely invitation.

It was now in the time of Carnival, when the Duke, who loved the company of ladies and dancing as much as any prince whosoever, made divers masks

---

[1] Charles Emanuel.

and balls, in which his own daughters, among divers other ladies, danced. And here it was his manner to place me always with his own hand near some fair lady, wishing us both to entertain each other with some discourse, which was a great favour among the Italians. He did many other ways also declare the great esteem he had of me without coming to any particular, the time of the year for going into the field being not yet come ; only he exercised his men often, and made them ready for his occasions in the spring.

The Duke at last resolving how to use my service, thought fit to send me to Languedoc, in France, to conduct four thousand men of the reformed religion, who had promised their assistance in his war, unto Piedmont. I willing accepted this offer ; so taking my leave of the Duke, and bestowing about seventy or eighty pounds among his officers, for the kind entertainment I had received, I took my leave also of my Lord Ambassador, and Sir Albertus Morton, who was likewise employed there, and prepared for my journey, for more expedition of which I was desired to go post. An old Scotch knight of the Sandilands hearing this, desired to borrow my horses as far as Heidelberg, which I granted, on condition that he would use them well by the way, and give them good keeping in that place afterwards.

The Count Scarnafissi was commanded to bear me company in this journey, and to carry with him some jewels, which he was to pawn in Lyons, in France, and with the money gotten for them to pay the soldiers above nominated ; for though the Duke had put extreme taxations on his people, insomuch that they paid not only a certain sum for every horse, ox, cow, or sheep that they kept, but afterwards for every chimney; and, finally, every single person by the poll, which amounted to a pistole, or 14s. a head or person, yet he wanted money; at which I did not so much wonder, as at the patience of his subjects; of whom I demanded, how they could bear their taxations? I have heard some of them answer, "We are not so much offended with the Duke for what he takes from us, as thankful for what he leaves us."

The Count Scarnafissi and I, now setting forth, rid post all day without eating or drinking by the way, the Count telling me still we should come to a good inn at night. It was now twilight, when the Count and I came near a solitary inn on the top of a mountain; the hostess, hearing the noise of horses, came out, with a child new-born on her left arm, and a rush candle in her hand. She presently knowing the Count de Scarnafissi, told him, "Ah, signior, you are come in a very ill time; the Duke's soldiers have been here to-day, and have left me nothing." I looked sadly upon the Count, when he, coming near to me, whispered me in the ear, and said, "It may be she thinks we will use her as the soldiers have done: go you into the house, and see whether you can find any thing; I will go round about the house, and perhaps I shall meet with some duck, hen, or chicken." Entering thus into the house, I found for all other furniture of it, the end of an old form, upon which sitting down, the hostess came towards me with a rush candle, and said, " I protest before God, that is true which I told the Count, here is nothing to eat ; but you are a gentleman, methinks it is pity you should want ; if you please, I will give you some milk out of my breasts, into a wooden dish I have here." This unexpected kindness made that impression on me, that I remember I was never so tenderly sensible of any thing. My answer was, " God forbid I should take away the milk from the child I see in thy arms : howbeit, I shall take it all my life for the greatest piece of charity that ever I heard of ;" and there-withal giving her a pistole, or a piece of gold of 14s., Scarnafissi and I got on horseback again, and rid another post, and came to an inn where we found very coarse cheer, yet hunger made us relish it.

In this journey I remember I went over Mount Gabelet by night, being carried down that precipice in a chair, a guide that went before bringing a bottle of straw with him, and kindling pieces of it from time to time, that we might see our way. Being at the bottom of a hill, I got on horseback and rid to Burgoine, resolving to rest there awhile ; and the rather, to speak truly, that I had heard divers say, and particularly Sir John Finnet,[1] and Sir Richard Newport,[2] that the host's daughter there was the handsomest woman that ever they saw in their lives. Coming to the inn, the Count Scarnafissi wished me to rest two or three hours, and he would go before to

---

[1] Master of the Ceremonies to James I.
[2] Herbert's relative.

Lyons, to prepare business for my journey to Languedoc. The host's daughter being not within, I told her father and mother that I desired only to see their daughter, as having heard her spoken of in England with so much advantage, that divers told me they thought her the handsomest creature that ever they saw. They answered, she was gone to a marriage, and should be presently sent for ; wishing me, in the mean while, to take some rest upon a bed, for they saw I needed it. Waking now about two hours afterwards, I found her sitting by me, attending when I would open mine eyes. I shall touch a little of her description ; her hair being of a shining black, was naturally curled in that order that a curious woman would have dressed it ; for one curl rising by degrees above another, and every bout tied with a small riband of a naccarine,[1] or the colour that the Knights of the Bath wear, gave a very graceful mixture, while it was bound up in this manner from the point of her shoulder to the crown of her head ; her eyes, which were round and black, seemed to be models of her whole beauty, and in some sort of her air, while a kind of light or flame came from them, not unlike that which the riband which tied up her hair exhibited ; I do not remember ever to have seen a prettier mouth, or whiter teeth ; briefly, all her outward parts seemed to become each other ; neither was there any thing that could be misliked, unless one should say her complexion was too brown, which yet,

---

[1] Pearl colour, Fr. *nacre*.

from the shadow, was heightened with a good blood in her cheeks. Her gown was a green Turkey grogram, cut all into panes or slashes, from the shoulder and sleeves unto the foot, and tied up at the distance of about a hand's-breadth everywhere with the same riband with which her hair was bound : so that her attire seemed as bizare as her person. I am too long in describing an host's daughter, howbeit I thought I might better speak of her than of divers other beauties held to be the best and fairest of the time, whom I have often seen. In conclusion, after about an hour's stay, I departed thence, without offering so much as the least incivility ; and indeed, after so much weariness, it was enough that her sight alone did somewhat refresh me.

From hence I went straight to Lyons. Entering the gate, the guards there, after their usual manner, demanded of me who I was, whence I came, and whither I went ? to which while I answered, I observed one of them look very attentively upon me, and then again upon a paper he had in his hand ; this having been done divers times, bred in me a suspicion that there was no good meaning in it, and I was not deceived in my conjecture ; for the Queen-mother of France having newly made an edict, no soldiers should be raised in France, the Marquis de Rambouillet,[1]

---

[1] Husband of Madame de Rambouillet, who received the wits and poets in the Hôtel de Rambouillet. Her daughter was Julie de Angennes, Duchesse de Montausier, known by Voiture's letters to her.

French ambassador at Turin, sent word of my employment to the Marquis de St. Chaumont, then
governor of Lyons, as also a description of my person.
This edict was so severe, as they who raised any men
were to lose their heads.

In this unfortunate conjuncture of affairs, nothing
fell out so well on my part, as that I had not raised
as yet any men; howbeit, the guards requiring me to
come before the governor, I went with them to a
church where he was at vespers; this while I walked
in the lower part of the church, little imagining what
danger I was in had I levied any men. I had not
walked there long, when a single person came to me,
apparelled in a black stuff suit, without any attendants
upon him, when I, supposing this person to be any
man rather than the governor, saluted him without
much ceremony. His first question was, whence I
came? I answered from Turin; he demanded then
whither I would go? I answered, I was not yet
resolved; his third question was, what news at Turin?
to which I answered, that I had no news to tell, as
supposing him to be only some busy or inquisitive
person. The Marquis hereupon called one of the
guards that conducted me thither, and after he had
whispered something in his ear, wished me to go
along with him, which I did willingly, as believing
this man would bring me to the governor. This man
silently leading me out of the church, brought me to a
fair house, into which I was no sooner entered, but he
told me I was commanded to prison there by him I
saw in the church, who was the governor; I replied,

I did not know him to be governor, nor that that was a prison, and that if I were out of it again, neither the governor nor all the town could bring me to it alive.

The master of the house hereupon spoke me very fair, and told me he would conduct me to a better chamber than any I could find in an inn, and thereupon conducted me to a very handsome lodging not far from the river. I had not been here half an hour when Sir Edward Sackville[1] (now Earl of Dorset) hearing only that an Englishman was committed, sent to know who I was, and why I was imprisoned. The governor not knowing whether to lay the fault upon my short answers to him, or my commission to levy men contrary to the queen's edict, made him so doubtful an answer (after he had a little touched upon both), as he dismissed him unsatisfied.

Sir Edward Sackville hereupon coming to the house where I was, as soon as ever he saw me, embraced me, saying, "Ned Herbert, what doest thou here?" I answered, "Ned Sackville, I am glad to see you; but I protest I know not why I am here." He again said, "Hast thou raised any men yet for the Duke of Savoy?" I replied, "Not so much as one;" then said he "I will warrant thee; though I must tell thee the governor is much offended at thy behaviour and language in the church. (I replied it was impossible for me to imagine him to be governor that came without a guard, and in such mean clothes as he then wore.) I will go to him again, and tell

---

[1] Known best for his duel with the Lord Bruce.

him what you say, and doubt not but you shall be suddenly freed." Hereupon returning to the governor, he told of what family I was, and of what condition, and that I had raised no men, and that I knew him not to be governor; whereupon the Marquis wished him to go back, that he would come in person to free me out of the house.

This message being brought me by Sir Edward Sackville, I returned this answer only; that it was enough if he sent order to free me. While these messages past, a company of handsome young men and women, out of I know not what civility, brought music under the window and danced before me, looking often up to see me; but Sir Edward Sackville being now returned with order to free me, I only gave them thanks out of the window, and so went along with them to the governor. Being come into a great hall where his lady was, and a large train of gentlewomen and other persons, the governor with his hat in his hand, demanded of me, whether I knew him? when his noble lady answering for me, said, "How could he know you, when you were in the church alone, and in this habit, being for the rest wholly a stranger to you?" which civility of hers, though I did not presently take notice of it, I did afterwards most thankfully acknowledge, when I was ambassador in France. The governor's next questions were the very same he made when he met me in the church; to which I made the very same answers before them all, concluding, that as I did not know him, he could think it no incongruity if I answered in those terms: the governor yet was not satisfied herewith, and his noble lady taking my part again, gave him those reasons for my answering him in that manner, that they silenced him from speaking any further. The governor turning back, I likewise, after an humble obeisance made to his lady, returned with Sir Edward Sackville to my lodgings.

This night I passed as quietly as I could, but the next morning advised with him what I was to do. I told him I had received a great affront, and that I intended to send him a challenge, in such courteous language that he could not refuse it. Sir Edward Sackville by all means dissuaded me from it; by which I perceived I was not to expect his assistance therein; and, indeed, the next day he went out of town.

Being alone now, I thought on nothing more than how to send him a challenge, which at last I penned to this effect: " That whereas he had given me great offence, without a cause, I thought myself bound as a gentleman to resent it, and therefore desired to see him with his sword in his hand in any place he should appoint; and hoped he would not interpose his authority as an excuse for not complying with his honour on this occasion, and that so I rested his humble servant."

Finding nobody in town for two or three days by whom I might send this challenge, I resolved, for my last means, to deliver it in person, and observe how he took it, intending to right myself as I could, when I found he stood upon his authority.

This night it happened that Monsieur Terant, formerly mentioned, came to the town; this gentleman knowing me well, and remembering our acquaintance both at France and Juliers, wished there were some occasion for him to serve me; I presently hereupon, taking the challenge out of my pocket, told him he would oblige me extremely, if he were pleased to deliver it; and that I hoped he might do it without danger, since I knew the French to be so brave a nation, that they would never refuse or dislike any thing that was done in an honourable and worthy way.

Terant took the challenge from me, and after he had read it, told me that the language was civil and discreet; nevertheless, he thought the governor would not return me that answer I expected; howsoever, said he, I will deliver it. Returning thus to my inn, and intending to sleep quieter that night than I had done three nights before; about one of the clock after midnight, I heard a great noise at my door, which awakened me, certain persons knocking so hard as if they would break it; besides, through the chinks thereof I saw light. This made me presently rise in my shirt, when, drawing my sword, I went to the door, and demanded who they were; and together told them, that if they came to make me prisoner, I would rather die with my sword in my hand; and therewithal opening the door, I found upon the stairs half a dozen men armed with halberts, whom I no sooner prepared to resist, but the chief of them told me, that they came not to me from the governor, but from my good friend the Duke of Montmorency, son to the duke

I formerly mentioned ; and that he came to town late that night, in his way from Languedoc (of which he was governor) to Paris ; and that he desired me, if I loved him, to rise presently and come to him, assuring me further that this was most true ; hereupon wishing them to retire themselves, I drest myself, and went with them.

They conducted me to the great hall of the governor, where the Duke of Montmorency and divers other cavaliers had been dancing with the ladies. I went presently to the Duke of Montmorency, who, taking me a little aside, told me that he had heard of the passage betwixt the governor and me, and that I had sent him a challenge ; howbeit, that he conceived men in his place were not bound to answer as private persons for those things they did by virtue of their office ; nevertheless, that I should have satisfaction in as ample manner as I could reasonably desire. Hereupon, bringing me with him to the governor, he freely told me, that now he knew who I was, he could do no less than assure me that he was sorry for what was done, and desired me to take this for satisfaction ; the Duke of Montmorency hereupon said presently, " *C'est assez ;* " it is enough. I then turning to him, demanded whether he would have taken this satisfaction in the like case ? He said, "Yes." After this, turning to the governor, I demanded the same question ; to which he answered, that he would have taken the same satisfaction, and less too. I kissing my hand, gave it to him, who embraced me, and so this business ended.

After some compliments passed between the Duke of Montmorency, who remembered the great love his father bore me, which he desired to continue in his person, and putting me in mind also of our being educated together for a while, demanded whether I would go with him to Paris? I told him that I was engaged to the Low Countries; but that wheresoever I was, I should be his most humble servant.

My employment with the Duke of Savoy in Languedoc being thus ended, I went from Lyons to Geneva, where I found also my fame had prevented[1] my coming; for the next morning after my arrival, the State taking notice of me, sent a messenger in their name to congratulate my being there, and presented me with some flagons of wine, desiring me (if I stayed there any while) to see their fortifications, and give my opinion of them; which I did, and told them I thought they were weakest where they thought themselves the strongest, which was on the hilly part, where, indeed, they had made great fortifications; yet, as it is a rule in war, that whatsoever may be made by art, may be destroyed by art again, I conceived they had need to fear the approach of an enemy on that part rather than any other. They replied, that divers great soldiers had told them the same; and that they would give the best order they could to serve themselves on that side.

Having rested here some while to take physic (my health being a little broken with long travel), I

---

[1] *i.e.,* preceded.

departed, after a fortnight's stay, to Basle, where taking a boat upon the river, I came at length to Strasburg, and from thence went to Heidelberg, where I was received again by the Prince Elector and Princess with much kindness, and viewed at leisure the fair library there, the gardens, and other rarities of that place; and here I found my horses I lent to Sandilands in good plight, which I then bestowed upon some servants of the prince, in way of retribution for my welcome thither. From hence Sir George Calvert[1] and myself went by water, for the most part, to the Low Countries, where taking leave of each other, I went straight to his excellency, who did extraordinarily welcome me, insomuch that it was observed that he did never outwardly make so much of any one as myself.

It happened this summer that the Low Country army was not drawn into the field, so that the Prince of Orange past his time at playing at chess with me after dinner; or in going to Ryswick with him to see his great horses; or in making love, in which, also, he used me as his companion, yet so, that I saw nothing openly, more than might argue a civil familiarity. When I was at any time from him, I did, by his good leave, endeavour to raise a troop of horse for the Duke of Savoy's service, as having obtained a commission to that purpose for my brother William, then an officer in the Low Country. Having these men in

---

[1] Afterwards Lord Baltimore.—*See* Catalogue of Royal and Noble Authors.

readiness, I sent word to the Count Scarnafissi thereof, who was now ambassador in England, telling him that if he would send money, my brother was ready to go.

Scarnafissi answered me, "That he expected money in England; and that as soon as he received it, he would send over so much as would pay a hundred horse;" but a peace betwixt him and the Spaniard being concluded not long after at Asti, the whole charge of keeping this horse fell upon me, without ever to this day receiving any recompense.

Winter now approaching, and nothing more to be done for that year, I went to the Brill to take shipping for England. Sir Edward Conway, who was then governor at that place, and afterwards secretary of state, taking notice of my being there, came to me, and invited me every day to come to him, while I attended only for a wind; which serving at last for my journey, Sir Edward Conway conducted me to the ship, into which, as soon as I was entered, he caused six pieces of ordnance to be discharged for my farewell. I was scarce gone a league into the sea, when the wind turned contrary, and forced me back again. Returning thus to the Brill, Sir Edward Conway welcomed me as before; and now, after some three or four days, the wind serving, he conducted me again to the ship, and bestowed six volleys of ordnance upon me. I was now about half way to England, when a most cruel storm arose, which tore our sails and spent our masts, insomuch that the master of our ship gave us all for lost, as the wind was extreme high, and together contrary. We were carried at last, though with much difficulty, back again to the Brill, where Sir Edward Conway did congratulate my escape; saying, he believed, certainly, that (considering the weather) I must needs be cast away.

After some stay here with my former welcome, the wind being now fair, I was conducted again to my ship by Sir Edward Conway, and the same volleys of shot given me, and was now scarce out of the haven, when the wind again turned contrary, and drove me back; this made me resolve to try my fortune here no longer; hiring a small bark therefore, I went to the sluice, and from thence to Ostend, where finding company, I went to Brussels.

In the inn where I lay, here an ordinary was kept, to which divers noblemen and principal officers of the Spanish army resorted; sitting among these at dinner, the next day after my arrival, no man knowing me or informing himself who I was, they fell into discourse of divers matters, in Italian, Spanish, and French; and at last three of them, one after another, began to speak of King James, my master, in a very scornful manner. I thought with myself then, that if I was a base fellow, I need not take any notice thereof, since no man knew me to be an Englishman, or that I did so much as understand their language; but my heart burning within me, I, putting off my hat, arose from the table, and turning myself to those that sat at the upper end, who had said nothing to the King my master's prejudice, I told them in Italian, "*Son Inglese;*" "I am an Englishman;" and should be unworthy to live if I suffered these words to be spoken of the King my master; and therewithal turning myself to those who had injured the King, I said, "You have spoken falsely, and I will fight with you all." Those at the upper end of the table finding I had so much reason on my part, did sharply check those I had questioned, and, to be brief, made them ask the King's forgiveness, wherewith also the King's health being drank round about the table, I departed thence to Dunkirk, and thence to Graveling, where I saw, though unknown, an English gentlewoman enter into a nunnery there.

I went thence to Calais; it was now extreme foul weather, and I could find no master of a ship willing to adventure to sea; howbeit, my impatience was such that I demanded of a poor fisherman there whether he would go, he answered, his ship was worse than any in the haven, as being open above, and without any deck, besides, that it was old; but, saith he, "I care for my life as little as you do, and if you will go, my boat is at your service."

I was now scarce out of the haven, when a high-grown sea had almost overwhelmed us, the waves coming in very fast into our ship, which we laded out again the best we could; notwithstanding which we expected every minute to be cast away: it pleased God yet before we were gone six leagues into the sea, to cease the tempest, and give us a fair passage over to the Downs, where after giving God thanks for my delivery from this most needless danger that ever I did run, I went to London.

I had not been here ten days when a quartan ague seized on me, which held me for a year and a-half without intermission, and a year and a-half longer at spring and fall; the good days I had during all this sickness I employed in study, the ill being spent in as sharp and long fits as I think ever any man endured, which brought me at last to be so lean and yellow, that scarce any man did know me.

It happened during this sickness, that I walked abroad one day towards Whitehall, where meeting with one Emerson, who spoke very disgraceful words of Sir Robert Harley, being then my dear friend, my weakness could not hinder me to be sensible of my friend's dishonour; shaking him therefore by a long beard he wore, I stept a little aside, and drew my sword in the street, Captain Thomas Scriven, a friend of mine, not being far off on one side, and divers friends of his on the other side. All that saw me wondered how I could go, being so weak and consumed as I was, but much more, that I would offer to fight; howsoever Emerson, instead of drawing his sword, ran away into Suffolk House, and afterwards informed the Lords of the Council of what I had done; who not long after sending for me, did not so much reprehend my taking part with my friend, as that I would adventure to fight, being in such a bad condition of health.

Before I came wholly out of my sickness, Sir George Villiers, afterwards Duke of Buckingham, came into the

King's favour. This cavalier meeting me accidentally at the Lady Stanhope's[1] house, came to me, and told me he had heard so much of my worth, as he would think himself happy if, by his credit with the king, he could do me any service; I humbly thanked him, but told him that for the present I had need of nothing so much as of health, but that if ever I had ambition I should take the boldness to make my address by him.

I was no sooner perfectly recovered of this long sickness, but the Earl of Oxford and myself resolved to raise two regiments for the service of the Venetians. While we were making ready for this journey, the king having an occasion to send an ambassador into France, required Sir George Villiers to present him with the names of the fittest men for that employment that he knew; whereupon eighteen names, among which mine was, being written in a paper, were presented to him; the King presently chose me, yet so as he desired first to have the approbation of his Privy Council, who, confirming his Majesty's choice, sent a messenger to my house among gardens, near the Old Exchange, requiring me to come presently to them. Myself little knowing then the honour intended me, asked the messenger "whether I had done any fault, that the lords sent for me so suddenly?" wishing him to tell the Lords that I was going to dinner, and would afterwards attend them. I had scarce dined, when

---

[1] Catherine, daughter of Francis Lord Hastings, first wife of Philip Lord Stanhope, afterwards Earl of Chesterfield.

another messenger was sent; this made me hasten to Whitehall, where I was no sooner come, but the Lords saluted me by the name of Lord Ambassador of France; I told their Lordships thereupon, that I was glad it was no worse, and that I doubted, that by their speedy sending for me, some complaint, though false, might be made against me.

My first commission was to renew the oath of alliance betwixt the two crowns, for which purpose I was Extraordinary Ambassador, which being done, I was to reside there as ordinary. I had received now about six or seven hundred pounds towards the charges of my journey, and locked it in certain coffers in my house, when, the night following, about one of the clock, I could hear divers men speak and knock at the door, in that part of the house where none did lie but myself, my wife, and her attendants; my servants being lodged in another house not far off. As soon as I heard the noise, I suspected presently they came to rob me of my money; howsoever, I thought fit to rise, and go to the window, to know who they were? The first word I heard was, "Darest thou come down, Welshman?" which I no sooner heard, but, taking a sword in one hand, and a little target in the other, I did in my shirt run down the stairs, open the doors suddenly, and charged ten or twelve of them with that fury that they ran away, some throwing away their halberts, others hurting their fellows, to make them go faster in a narrow way they were to pass; in which disordered manner I drove them to the middle of the street by the

Exchange, where, finding my bare feet hurt by the stones I trod on, I thought fit to return home, and leave them to their flight. My servants, hearing the noise, by this time were got up, and demanded whether I would have them pursue those rogues that fled away ; but I answering that I thought they were out of their reach, we returned home together.

While I was preparing myself for my journey, it happened that I passing through the Inner Temple one day, and encountering Sir Robert Vaughan in this country, some harsh words passed betwixt us, which occasioned him, at the persuasion of others whom I will not nominate, to send me a challenge. This was brought me at my house in Blackfriars, by Captain Charles Price, upon a Sunday, about one of the clock in the afternoon. When I had read it, I told Charles Price that I did ordinarily bestow this day in devotion, nevertheless, that I would meet Sir Robert Vaughan presently, and gave him thereupon the length of my sword, demanding whether he brought any second with him ; to which Charles Price replying, that he would be in the field with him, I told my brother, Sir Henry Herbert, then present, thereof, who readily offering himself to be my second, nothing was wanting now but the place to be agreed upon betwixt us, which was not far from the waterside, near Chelsea.

My brother and I taking boat presently, to the place, where, after we had stayed about two hours in vain, I desired my brother to go to Sir Robert Vaughan's lodging, and tell him that I now attended his coming a great while, and that I desired him to come away speedily; hereupon my brother went, and after a while returning back again, he told me they were not ready yet. I attended then about an hour and a half longer; but as he did not come yet, I sent my brother a second time to call him away, and to tell him I catched cold, nevertheless that I would stay there till sunset: my brother yet could not bring him along, but returned himself to the place, where we stayed together till half an hour after sunset, and then returned home.

The next day the Earl of Worcester,[1] by the King's command, forbid me to receive any message or letter from Sir Robert Vaughan, and advertised me withal, that the King had given him charge to end the business betwixt us; for which purpose he desired me to come before him the next day about two of the clock; at which time, after the Earl had told me, that being now made ambassador, and a public person, I ought not to entertain private quarrels; after which, without much ado, he ended the business betwixt Sir Robert Vaughan and myself. It was thought by some that this would make me lose my place, I being under so great an obligation to the King for my employment in France; but Sir George Villiers, afterwards Duke of Buckingham, told me he would warrant me for this one time, but I must do so no more.

---

[1] Edward Somerset, Earl of Worcester, Lord Privy Seal, and Knight of the Garter.

I was now almost ready for my journey, and had received already as choice a company of gentlemen for my attendants, as, I think, ever followed an ambassador; when some of my private friends told me, that I was not to trust so much to my pay from the Exchequer, but that it was necessary for me to take letters of credit with me, for as much money as I could well procure. Informing myself hereupon who had furnished the last ambassador, I was told Monsieur Savage, a Frenchman; coming to his house I demanded whether he would help me with moneys in France, as he had done the last ambassador? He said he did not know me, but would inform himself better who I was: departing thus from him, I went to Signior Burlamacchi, a man of great credit in those times, and demanded of him the same; his answer was, that he knew me to be a man of honour, and I had kept my word with every body; whereupon also, going to his study, gave me a letter of credit to one Monsieur de Langherac, in Paris, for 2000l. sterling. I then demanded what security he expected for this money? he said he would have nothing but my promise; I told him he had put a great obligation upon me, and that I would strive to acquit myself of it the best I could.

Having now a good sum of money in my coffers, and this letter of credit, I made ready for my journey. The day I went out of London, I remember, was the same in which Queen Anne was carried to burial; which was a sad spectacle to all that had occasion to honour her. My first night's journey was to Gravesend, where, being at supper in my inn, Monsieur Savage, formerly mentioned, came to me, and told me, that whereas I had spoken to him for a letter of credit, he had made one which he thought would be to my contentment. I demanded to whom it was directed; he said, to Monsieur Tallemant and Rambouillet, in Paris: I asked then, what they were worth? he said, above one hundred thousand pounds sterling. I demanded for how much this letter of credit was? he said, for as much as I should have need of; I asked what security he required? he said, nothing but my word, which he had heard was inviolable.

From Gravesend, by easy journeys, I went to Dover, where I took shipping, with a train of a hundred and odd persons,[1] and arrived shortly after at Calais, where I remember my cheer was twice as good as at Dover, and my reckoning half as cheap; from whence I went to Boulogne, Monstreville, Abbeville, Amiens, and in two days, thence to St. Dennis, near Paris, where I was met with a great train of coaches, that were sent to receive me; as also by the master of the ceremonies, and Monsieur Mennon,[2] my fellow scholar, with Monsieur Disancourt, who then kept an academy, and brought with him a brave company of gentlemen on great horses, to attend me into town.

It was now somewhat late when I entered Paris, upon a Saturday night; I was but newly settled in

---

[1] Thomas Carew, the poet, went as Lord Herbert's Secretary.
[2] Or, *de Menou.*

my lodging, when a secretary of the Spanish ambassador there told me that his lord desired to have the first audience from me, and therefore requested he might see me the next morning. I replied, it was a day I gave wholly to devotion ; and therefore entreated him to stay till some more convenient time. The secretary replied, that his master did hold it not less holy ; howbeit, that his respect to me was such, that he would prefer the desire he had to serve me before all other considerations ; howsoever, I put him off until Monday following.

Not long after, I took a house in Faubourg St. Germain, Rue Tournon, which cost me two hundred pounds sterling yearly. Having furnished the house richly, and lodged all my train, I prepared for a journey to Tours and Touraine, where the French court then was. Being come hither in extreme hot weather, I demanded audience of the King and Queen,[1] which being granted, I did assure the King of the great affection the King my master bore him, not only out of the ancient alliance betwixt the two crowns, but because Henry the Fourth and the King my master had stipulated with each other, that whensoever any one of them died, the survivor should take care of the other's child. I assured him further, that no charge was so much imposed upon me by my instructions, as that I should do good offices betwixt both kingdoms ; and therefore, that it

---

[1] Louis XII., son of Henry IV. Anne of Austria, mother of Louis XIV.

were a great fault in me, if I behaved myself otherwise than with all respect to his Majesty. This being done, I presented to the King a letter of credence from the King my master. The King assured me of a reciprocal affection to the King my master, and of my particular welcome to his court; his words were never many, as being so extreme a stutterer, that he would sometimes hold his tongue out of his mouth a good while, before he could speak so much as one word; he had, besides, a double row of teeth, and was observed seldom or never to spit, or blow his nose, or to sweat much, though he were very laborious, and almost indefatigable in his exercises of hunting and hawking, to which he was much addicted; neither did it hinder him, though he was burst in his body, as we call it, or herniosus; for he was noted in those sports, though oftentimes on foot, to tire not only his courtiers, but even his lackeys, being equally insensible, as was thought, either of heat or cold.

His understanding and natural parts were as good as could be expected in one that was brought up in so much ignorance, which was on purpose so done, that he might be the longer governed; howbeit, he acquired in time a great knowledge in affairs, as conversing for the most part with wise and active persons. He was noted to have two qualities incident to all who were ignorantly brought up—suspicion and dissimulation; for as ignorant persons walk so much in the dark, they cannot be exempt from the fear of stumbling; and as they are likewise deprived of, or deficient in those true principles by which they should govern both public and private actions in a wise, solid, and demonstrative way, they strive commonly to supply these imperfections with covert arts, which, although it may be sometimes excusable in necessitous persons, and be indeed frequent among those who negotiate in small matters, yet condemnable in Princes, who, proceeding upon foundations of reason and strength, ought not to submit themselves to such poor helps. Howbeit, I must observe, that neither his fears did take away his courage, when there was occasion to use it, nor his dissimulation extend itself to the doing of private mischiefs to his subjects, either of one or the other religion. His favourite was one Monsieur de Luynes, who in his nonage gained much upon the King, by making hawks fly at all little birds in his gardens, and by making some of those little birds again catch butterflies; and had the King used him for no other purpose, he might have been tolerated; but as, when the King came to a riper age, the government of public affairs was drawn chiefly from his counsels, not a few errors were committed.

The Queen-mother, princes, and nobles of that kingdom repined that his advices to the King should be so prevalent, which also at least caused a civil war in that kingdom. How unfit this man was for the credit he had with the King may be argued by this; that when there was a question made about some business in Bohemia, he demanded whether it was an inland country, or lay upon the sea? And thus much for the present of the King and his favourite.

After my audience with the King, I had another from the Queen, being sister to the King of Spain; I had little to say unto her, but some compliments on the King my master's part, but such compliments as her sex and quality were capable of. This Queen was exceedingly fair, like those of the house of Austria, and together of so mild and good a condition, she was never noted to have done ill offices to any, but to have mediated as much as was possible for her, in satisfaction of those who had any suit with the King, as far as their cause would bear. She had now been married divers years without having any children, though so ripe for them, that nothing seemed to be wanting on her part. I remember her the more particularly, that she shewed publicly at my audiences that favour to me, as not only my servants but divers others took notice of it.

After this, my first audience, I went to see Monsieur Luynes, and the principal ministers of state, as also the princes and princesses, and ladies then in the court, and particularly the Princess of Conti, from whom I carried the scarf formerly mentioned; and this is as much as I shall declare in this place, concerning my negotiation with the King and state, my purpose being, if God sends me life, to set them forth apart, as having the copies of all my despatches in a great trunk in my house in London; and considering that in the time of my stay there, there were divers civil wars in that country, and that the Prince, now King, passed with my Lord of Buckingham and others through France into Spain; and the business of the

Elector Palatine in Bohemia, and the battle of Prague, and divers other memorable accidents, both of state and war, happened during the time of my employment; I conceive a narration of them may be worth the seeing, to them who have it not from a better hand; I shall only therefore relate here, as they come into my memory, certain little passages, which may serve in some part to declare the history of my life.

Coming back from Tours to Paris, I gave the best order I could concerning the expenses of my house, family, and stable, that I might settle all things as near as was possible in a certain course, allowing, according to the manner of France, so many pounds of beef, mutton, veal, and pork, and so much also in turkeys, capons, pheasants, partridges, and all other fowls, as also pies and tarts, after the French manner, and after all this a dozen dishes of sweetmeats every day constantly. The ordering of these things was the heavier to me, that my wife flatly refused to come over into France, as being now entered into a dropsy, which also had kept her without children for many years; I was constrained therefore to make use of a steward, who was understanding and diligent, but no very honest man. My chief secretary was William Boswell, now the King's agent in the Low Countries; my secretary for the French tongue was one Monsieur Ozier, who afterwards was the King's agent in France. The gentleman of my horse was Monsieur de Meny,[1] who afterwards commanded a thousand horse in the

---

[1] Perhaps de Menou.

wars of Germany, and proved a very gallant gentleman; Mr. Crofts was one of my principal gentlemen,
and afterwards made the king's cupbearer; and Thomas
Carew, that excellent wit, the King's carver; Edmund
Taverner, whom I made my under-secretary, was
afterwards chief secretary to the Lord Chamberlain;
and one Mr. Smith, secretary to the Earl of Northumberland; I nominate these, and could many more,
that came to very good fortunes afterwards, because
I may verify that which I said before concerning the
gentlemen that attended me.

When I came to Paris the English and French were
in very ill intelligence with each other, insomuch
that one Buckly coming then to me, said he was
assaulted and hurt upon Pontneuf, only because he
was an Englishman; nevertheless, after I had been
in Paris about a month, all the English were so
welcome thither, that no other nation was so acceptable
amongst them, insomuch that my gentlemen having a
quarrel with some debauched French, who in their
drunkenness quarrelled with them, divers principal
gentlemen of that nation offered themselves to assist
my people with their swords.

It happened one day, that my cousin, Oliver
Herbert, and George Radney, being gentlemen who
attended me, and Henry Whittingham, my butler, had
a quarrel with some French, upon I know not what
frivolous occasion. It happened my cousin, Oliver
Herbert, had for his opposite a fencer belonging to
the Prince of Condé, who was dangerously hurt by
him in divers places; but as the house, or hostel, of

the Prince of Condé was not far off, and himself well beloved in those quarters, the French in great multitudes arising, drove away the three above mentioned into my house, pursuing them within the gates. I, perceiving this at a window, ran out with my sword, which the people no sooner saw, but they fled again as fast as ever they entered; howsoever, the Prince of Condé his fencer was in that danger of his life, that Oliver Herbert was forced to fly France, which, that he might do the better, I paid the said fencer two hundred crowns, or sixty pounds sterling, for his hurt and cures.

The plague now being hot in Paris, I desired the Duke of Montmorency to lend me the castle of Merlou, where I lived in the time of his most noble father, which he willingly granted. Removing thither, I enjoyed that sweet place and country, wherein I found not a few that welcomed me out of their ancient acquaintance.

On the one side of me was the Baron de Montaterre, of the reformed religion, and Monsieur de Bouteville on the other, who, though young at that time, proved afterwards to be that brave cavalier which all France did so much celebrate. In both their castles, likewise, were ladies of much beauty and discretion, and particularly a sister of Bouteville, thought to be one of the chief perfections of the time, whose company yielded some divertisement when my public occasions did suffer it.

Winter being now come, I returned to my house in Paris, and prepared for renewing the oath of alliance

betwixt the two crowns, for which, as I said formerly,
I had an extraordinary commission ; nevertheless, the
king put off the business to as long a time as he well
could. In the meanwhile, Prince Henry of Nassau,
brother to Prince Maurice, coming to Paris, was met
and much welcomed by me, as being obliged to him,
no less than to his brother in the Low Countries.
This Prince, and all his train, were feasted by me at
Paris with a hundred dishes, costing, as I remember,
in all, one hundred pounds.

The French King at last resolving upon a day for
performing the ceremony betwixt the two crowns
above mentioned, myself and all my train put ourselves into that sumptuous equipage, that I remember
it cost me one way or another above one thousand
pounds. And truly the magnificence of it was such,
as a little French book was presently printed thereof.
This being done, I resided here in the quality of an
ordinary ambassador.

And now I shall mention some particular passages
concerning myself, without entering yet any way into
the whole frame and context of my negotiation,
reserving them, as I said before, to a particular
treatise. I spent my time much in the visits of the
princes, council of state, and great persons of the
French kingdom, who did ever punctually requite my
visits. The like I did also to the chief ambassadors
there, among whom, the Venetian, Low Country,
Savoy, and the united princes in Germany, ambassadors, did bear me that respect, that they usually
met in my house, to advise together concerning the

great affairs of that time; for as the Spaniard then was so potent, that he seemed to affect a universal monarchy, all the above mentioned ambassadors did, in one common interest, strive to oppose him.

All our endeavours yet could not hinder, but that he both publicly prevailed in his attempts abroad, and privately did corrupt divers of the principal ministers of state in this kingdom. I came to discover this by many ways, but by none more effectually than by the means of an Italian, who returned over, by letters of exchange, the moneys the Spanish ambassador received for his occasions in France; for I perceived that when the said Italian was to receive any extraordinary great sum for the Spanish ambassador's use, the whole face of affairs was presently changed, insomuch that neither my reasons, nor the ambassadors above mentioned, how valid soever, could prevail; though yet afterwards we found means together to reduce affairs to their former train, till some other new great sum coming to the Spanish ambassador's hand, and from thence to the aforesaid ministers of state, altered all.

Howbeit, divers visits passed betwixt the Spanish ambassador and myself, in one of which he told me, that though our interests were divers, yet we might continue friendship in our particular persons; " For," said he, " it can be no occasion of offence betwixt us, that each of us strive the best he can to serve the king his master." I disliked not his reasons, though yet I could not omit to tell him that I would maintain the dignity of the King my master the best I could ; and this I said, because the Spanish ambassador had taken place of the English in the time of Henry IV. in this fashion : they both meeting in an antechamber to the Secretary of State, the Spanish ambassador, leaning to the wall in that posture that he took the hand of the English ambassador, said publicly, " I hold this place in the right of the King my master ; " which small punctilio being not resented by our ambassador at that time, gave the Spaniard occasion to brag that he had taken the hand from our ambassador.

This made me more watchful to regain the honour which the Spaniard pretended to have gotten herein ; so that though the ambassador, in his visits, often repeated the words above mentioned, being in Spanish, " *Que cada uno haga lo que pudiere por su amo ;* " " Let every man do the best he can for his master ; " I attended the occasion to right my master.

It happened one day, that both of us going to the French King for our several affairs, the Spanish ambassador, between Paris and Estampes, being upon his way before me in his coach, with a train of about sixteen or eighteen persons on horseback, I following him in my coach, with about ten or twelve horse, found that either I must go the Spanish pace, which is slow, or if I hasted to pass him, that I must hazard the suffering of some affront like unto that our former ambassador received ; proposing hereupon to my gentlemen the whole business, I told them that I meant to redeem the honour of the King my master some way or other, demanding further, whether they would assist me? which they promising, I bid the coachman drive on.

The Spanish ambassador seeing me approach, and imagining what my intention was, sent a gentleman to me, to tell me he desired to salute me; which I accepting, the gentleman returned to the ambassador, who, alighting from his coach, attended me in the middle of the highway; which being perceived by me, I alighted also, when some extravagant compliments having passed betwixt us, the Spanish ambassador took his leave of me, went to a dry ditch not far off, upon pretence of making water, but indeed to hold the upper hand of me while I passed by in my coach; which being observed by me, I left my coach, and getting upon a spare horse I had there, rode into the said dry ditch, and telling him aloud, that I knew well why he stood there, bid him afterwards get to his coach, for I must ride that way; the Spanish ambassador, who understood me well, went to his coach grumbling and discontented, although yet neither he nor his train did any more than look one upon another in a confused manner; my coach this while passing by the ambassador on the same side I was, I shortly after left my horse and got into it. It happened this while, that one of my coach horses having lost a shoe, I thought fit to stay at a smith's forge, about a quarter of a mile before; this shoe could not be put on so soon, but that the Spanish ambassador overtook us, and might indeed have passed us, but that he thought I would give him another affront. Attending, therefore, the smith's leisure, he stayed on the highway, to our no little admiration, until my horse was shod. We continued our journey to Estampes, the Spanish ambassador following us still at a good distance.

I should scarce have mentioned this passage, but that the Spaniards do so much stand upon their *pundonores*[1]; for confirming whereof I have thought fit to remember the answer a Spanish ambassador made to Philip II., King of Spain, who finding fault with him for neglecting a business of great importance in Italy, because he could not agree with the French ambassador about some such *pundonore* as this, said to him, "*Como ha dejado una cosa de importancia por una ceremonia !*" "How have you left a business of importance for a ceremony !" The ambassador boldly replied to his master, "*Como por una ceremonia ! Vuesa Majestad misma no es sino una ceremonia ;*" "How, for a ceremony! Your Majesty's self is but a ceremony."

Howsoever, the Spanish ambassador taking no notice publicly of the advantage I had of him herein, dissembled it, as I heard, till he could find some fit occasion to resent this passage, which yet he never did to this day.

Among the visits I rendered to the grandees of France, one of the principal I made was to that brave general the Duke of Lesdiguères, who was now grown very old and deaf. His words to me were, "Monsieur, you must do me the honour to speak high, for I am deaf;" my answer to him was, "You was born to

---

[1] Nice points of behaviour, punctillos. —*Sp.*

command not to obey; it is enough if others have ears to hear you." This compliment took him much, and indeed I have a manuscript of his military precepts and observations, which I value at a great price.

I shall relate now some things concerning myself, which though they may seem scarcely credible, yet, before God, are true. I had been now in France about a year and a half, when my tailor, Andrew Henly of Basle, who lives in Blackfriars, demanded of me half a yard of satin, to make me a suit, more than I was accustomed to give, of which I required a reason, saying, I was not fatter now than when I came to France. He answered it was true, but you are taller; whereunto when I would give no credit, he brought his old measures, and made it appear that they did not reach to their just places. I told him I knew not how this happened, but however he should have a half a yard more, and that when I came to England I would clear the doubt, for a little before my departure thence, I remember William Earl of Pembroke and myself did measure heights together, at the request of the Countess of Bedford, and he was then higher than I by about the growth of my little finger; at my return, therefore, into England, I measured again with the same Earl, and, to both our great wonders, found myself taller than he by the breadth of a little finger; which breadth of mine I could attribute to no other cause but to my quartan ague formerly mentioned, which, when it quitted me, left me in a more perfect health than I formerly enjoyed, and indeed disposed me to some follies which I afterwards repented and do still repent of; but as my wife refused to come over, and my temptations were great, I hope the faults I committed are the more pardonable; howsoever, I can say, truly, that whether in France or England, I was never in a bawdy-house, nor used my pleasures intemperately, and much less did accompany them with that dissimulation and falsehood which is commonly found in men addicted to love women.

To conclude this passage, which I unwillingly mention, I must protest again, before God, that I never delighted in that or any other sin, and that if I transgressed sometimes in this kind, it was to avoid a greater ill; for certainly if I had been provided with a lawful remedy, I should have fallen into no extravagancy. I could extenuate my fault by telling circumstances which would have operated, I doubt, upon the chastest of mankind; but I forbear, those things being not fit to be spoken of; for though the philosophers have accounted this act to be *inter honesta factu*, where neither injury nor violence was offered, yet they ever reckoned it among the *turpia dictu*. I shall therefore only tell some other things alike strange of myself.

I weighed myself in balances often with men lower than myself by the head, and in their bodies slenderer, and yet was found lighter than they, as Sir John Danvers, knight, and Richard Griffiths, now living, can witness, with both whom I have been weighed. I had also, and have still a pulse on the crown of my head. It is well known to those that wait in my chamber, that the shirts, waistcoats, and other garments I wear next my body, are sweet, beyond what either can easily be believed, or hath been observed in any else, which sweetness also was found to be in my breath above others, before I used to take tobacco, which towards my latter time I was forced to take against certain rheums and catarrhs that trouble me, which yet did not taint my breath for any long time; I scarce ever felt cold in my life, though yet so subject to catarrhs, though I think no man ever was more obnoxious to it; all which I do in a familiar way mention to my posterity, though otherwise they might be thought scarce worth the writing.

The effect of my being sent into France by the King my master, being to hold all good intelligence betwixt both crowns, my employment was more noble and pleasing, and my pains not great, France having no design at that time upon England, and King James being that pacific prince all the world knew. And thus, besides the times I spent in treaties and nego- tiations, I had either with the ministers of state in France, or foreign ambassadors residing in Paris, I had spare time not only for my book, but for visits to divers grandees, for little more ends than obtain- ing some intelligence of the affairs of that kingdom, and civil conversation, for which their free, generous, and cheerful company was no little motive; persons of all quality being so addicted to have mutual enter- tainment with each other, that in calm weather one might find all the noble and good company in Paris, of both sexes, either in the garden of the Tuileries, or in the park of Bois de Vincennes, they thinking it almost an incivility to refuse their presence and free discourse to any who were capable of coming to those places, either under the recommendation of good parts, or but so much as handsome clothes and a good equipage. When foul weather was, they spent their time in visits at each others' houses, where they interchanged civil discourses, or heard music, or fell to dancing, using, according to the manner of that country, all the reasonable liberties they could with their honour; while their manner was, either in the garden of the Tuileries, or elsewhere, if any one discoursing with a lady did see some other of good fashion approach to her, he would leave her and go to some other lady, he who conversed with her at that time quitting her also, and going to some other, that so addresses might be made equal and free to all without scruple on any part, neither was exception made, or quarrel begun, upon these terms.

It happened one day, that I being ready to return from the Tuileries, about eight of the clock in the summer, with intention to write a dispatch to the King about some intelligence I had received there, the Queen, attended with her principal ladies, without so much as one cavalier, did enter the garden. I staid on one side of an alley, there to do my reverence to her and the rest, and so return to my house, when the Queen perceiving me, staid awhile, as if she expected I should attend her; but as I stirred not more than to give her that great respect I owed her, the Princess of Conti, who was next, called me to her, and said I must go along with her, but I excusing myself upon occasion of a present dispatch which I was to make unto his Majesty, the Duchess of Ventadour, who followed her, came to me, and said I must not refuse her ; whereupon, leading her by her arms, according to the manner of that country, the Princess of Conti, offended that I had denied her that civility which I had yielded to another, took me off after she had demanded the consent of the Duchess ; but the Queen then also staying, I left the Princess, and, with all due humility, went to the Queen, and led her by the arms ; walking thus to a place in the garden where some orange trees grew, and here discoursing with her Majesty bare-headed, some small shot fell on both our heads ; the occasion whereof was this. The King being in the garden, and shooting at a bird in the air, which he did with much perfection, the descent of his shot fell just upon us ; the Queen was much startled herewith, when I, coming nearer to her, demanded whether she had received any harm ; to which she answering no, and therewith taking two or three small pellets from her hair, it was thought fit to send a gardener to the King, to tell him that her Majesty was there, and that he should shoot no more that way, which was no sooner heard among the nobles that attended him, but many of them leaving him, came to the Queen and ladies, among whom was Monsieur le Grand,[1] who, finding the Queen still discoursing with me, stole behind her, and letting fall gently some comfits he had in his pocket upon the Queen's hair, gave her occasion to apprehend that some shot had

---

[1] Roger, Duc de Bellegarde, *grand ecuyer* under Henry III.

fallen on her again. Turning hereupon to Monsieur le Grand, I said that I marvelled that so old a courtier as he was, could find no means to entertain ladies but by making them afraid ; but the Queen shortly after returning to her lodging, I took my leave of her, and came home. All which passage I have thought fit to set down, the accident above mentioned being so strange, that it can hardly be paralleled.

It fell out one day that the Prince of Condé coming to my house, some speech happened concerning the King my master, in whom, though he acknowledged much learning, knowledge, clemency, and divers other virtues, yet he said he had heard that the King was much given to cursing, I answered that it was out of his gentleness ; but the Prince demanding how cursing could be a gentleness ? I replied, " Yes, for though he could punish men himself, yet he left them to God to punish ;" which defence of the King my master was afterwards much celebrated in the French court.

Monsieur de Luynes continuing still the King's favourite, advised him to war against his subjects of the reformed religion in France ; saying, he would neither be a great prince as long as he suffered so puissant a party to remain within his dominions, nor could justly style himself the most Christian King, as long as he permitted such heretics to be in that great number they were, or to hold those strong places which by public edict were assigned to them ; and therefore, that he should extirpate them as the Spaniards had done the Moors, who are all banished into other countries, as we may find in their histories.

This counsel, though approved by the young King, was yet disliked by other grave and wise persons about him, and particularly by the chancellor Sillery, and the president Jeannin, who thought better to have a peace which had two religions, than a war that had none. Howbeit, the design of Luynes was applauded, not only by the Jesuit party in France, but by some princes and other martial persons, insomuch that the Duke of Guise[1] coming to see me one day, said that they should never be happy in France, until those of the religion were rooted out. I answered that I wondered to hear him say so, and the Duke demanding why? I replied that whensoever those of the religion were put down, the turn of the great persons, and governors of provinces of that kingdom would be next; and that, though the present King was a good prince, yet that their successors may be otherwise, and that men did not know how soon princes might prove tyrants when they had nothing to fear; which speech of mine was fatal, since those of the religion were no sooner reduced into that weak condition into which now they are, but the governors of provinces were brought lower, and curbed much in their power and authority, and the Duke of Guise first of them all; so that I doubt not but my words were well remembered.

Howsoever, the war now went on with much fervour; neither could I dissuade it, though using, according to the instructions I had from the King my master,

---

[1] Charles, son of Henry Duke of Guise who was killed at Blois.

many arguments for that purpose. I was told often, that if the reformation in France had been like that in England, where they observed we retained the hierarchy, together with decent rites and ceremonies in the church, as also holidays in the memory of saints, music in churches, and divers other testimonies, both of glorifying God and giving honour and reward to learning, they could much better have tolerated it, but such a rash and violent reformation as theirs was, ought by no means to be approved; whereunto I answered, that though the causes of departing from the Church of Rome were taught and delivered by many sober and modest persons, yet that the reformation in great part was acted by the common people, whereas ours began at the prince of state, and therefore was more moderate; which reason I found did not displease them: I added further then, that the reformed religion in France would easily enough admit an hierarchy, if they had sufficient means among them to maintain it, and that if their churches were as fair as those which the Roman Catholics had, they would use the more decent sorts of rites and ceremonies, and together like well of organs and choirs of singers, rather than make a breach or schism on that occasion. As for holidays, I doubted not but the principal persons and ministers of their religion would approve it much better than the common people, who, being labourers and artizans for the most part, had the advantages for many more days, than the Roman Catholic for getting their living; howsoever, that those of the religion had been good cautions to make the Roman Catholic priests, if not better, yet at least more wary in their lives and actions ; it being evident that since the reformation began among those of the religion, the Roman Catholics had divers ways reformed themselves, and abated not only much of their power they usurped over laics, but were more pious and continent than formerly. Lastly, that those of the religion acknowledged solely the King's authority in government of all affairs ; whereas the other side held the regal power not only inferior in divers points, but subordinate to the papal : nothing of which yet served to divert Monsieur de Luynes, or the King, from their resolutions.

The King having now assembled an army, and made some progress against those of the religion, I had instruction sent me from the King my master to mediate a peace, and if I could not prevail therein, to use some such words as may both argue his Majesty's care of them of the religion, and together, to let the French King know, that he would not permit their total ruin and extirpation. The King was now going to lay siege to Saint-Jean-d'Angély, when myself was newly recovered of a fever at Paris, in which besides the help of many able physicians, I had the comfort of divers visits from many principal grandees of France, and particularly the Princess of Conti, who would sit by my bedside two or three hours, and with cheerful discourse entertain me, though yet I was brought so low, that I could scarce return any thing by way of answer, but thanks.

The command yet which I received from the King

my master quickened me, insomuch that by slow degrees I went into my coach, together with my train, towards Sant-Jean-d'Angély. Being arrived within a small distance of that place, I found by divers circumstances, that the effect of my negotiation had been discovered from England, and that I was not welcome thither; howbeit, having obtained an audience from the King, I exposed what I had in charge to say to him, to which yet I received no other answer but that I should go to Monsieur de Luynes, by whom I should know his Majesty's intention.

Repairing thus to him, I did find outwardly good reception, though yet I did not know how cunningly he proceeded to betray and frustrate my endeavours for those of the religion; for, hiding a gentleman called Monsieur Arnauld[1] behind the hangings in his chamber, who was then of the religion, but had promised a revolt to the King's side, this gentleman, as he himself confessed afterwards to the Earl of Carlisle, had in charge to relate unto those of the religion, how little help they might expect from me, when he should tell them the answers which Monsieur de Luynes made me. Sitting thus in a chair before Monsieur de Luynes, he demanded the effect of my business? I answered, that the King my master commanded me to mediate a peace betwixt his Majesty and his subjects of the religion, and that I desired to do it in all those fair and equal terms

---

[1] Son of Anthoine de la Mothe-Arnauld. The father was a Protestant, but not the son.—DE RÉMUSAT.

which might stand with the honour of France and the good intelligence betwixt the two kingdoms : to which he returned this rude answer only ; "What hath the King your master to do with our actions? why doth he meddle with our affairs ?"

My reply was, "That the King my master ought not to give an account of the reason which induced him hereunto, and for me it was enough to obey him ; howbeit, if he did ask me in more gentle terms, I should do the best I could to give him satisfaction ;" to which, though he answered no more than the word *bien*, or "well," I, pursuing my instruction, said "that the King my master, according to the mutual stipulation betwixt Henry IV. and himself, that the survivor of either of them should procure the tranquillity and peace of the other's estate, had sent this message ; and that he had not only testified this his pious inclination heretofore in the late civil wars of France, but was desirous on this occasion also to shew how much he stood affected to the good of the kingdom ; besides, he hoped that when peace was established here, that the French King might be the more easily disposed to assist the Palatine, who was an ancient friend and ally of the French crown."

His reply to this was, "We will have none of your advices ;" whereupon I said, that I took these words for an answer, and was sorry only that they did not understand sufficiently the affection and good-will of the King my master ; and since they rejected it upon those terms, I had in charge to tell him, that we knew very well what we had to do. Luynes, seeming offended herewith, said, "*Nous ne vous craignons pas*," or, "We are not afraid of you :" I replied hereupon, that, "if you had said you had not loved us, I should have believed you, but should have returned you another answer;" in the mean while that I had no more to say than what I told you formerly, which was, that we knew what we had to do.

This, though somewhat less than was in my instructions, so angered him, that in much passion he said, "*Par Dieu, si vous n'étiez Monsieur l'Ambassadeur, je vous traiterais d'un autre sorte;*" "By God, if you were not Monsieur Ambassador, I would use you after another fashion." My answer was, that as I was an ambassador, so I was also a gentleman; and therewithal laying my hand upon the hilt of my sword, told him, there was that which should make him an answer, and so arose from my chair; to which Monsieur de Luynes made no reply, but arising likewise from his chair, offered civilly to accompany me to the door; but I telling him there was no occasion for him to use ceremony after so rude an entertainment, I departed from him.

From thence returning to my lodging, I spent three or four days afterwards in seeing the manner of the French discipline, in making approaches to towns; at what time I remember, that going in my coach within reach of cannon, those in the town imagining me to be an enemy, made many shots against me, which so affrighted my coachman, that he durst drive no farther; whereupon alighting, I bid him put the horses out of danger; and notwithstanding many more shots made against me, went on foot to the trenches, where one Seaton, a Scotchman, conducting me, shewed me their works, in which I found little differing from the Low Country manner.

Having satisfied myself in this manner, I thought fit to take my leave of the King, being at Cognac, the city of Saint-Jean-d'Angély being now surrendered unto him. Coming thus to a village not far from Cognac, about ten of the clock at night, I found all the lodgings possessed by soldiers, so that alighting in the market-place, I sent my servants to the inns to get some provision, who bringing me only six rye loaves, which I was doubtful whether I should bestow on myself and company, or on my horses, Monsieur de Ponts, a French nobleman of the religion, attended with a brave train, hearing of my being there, offered me lodging in his castle near adjoining.

I told him it was a great courtesy at that time, yet I could not with my honour accept it, since I knew it would endanger him, my business to those parts being in favour of those of the religion, and the chief ministers of state in France being jealous of my holding intelligence with him; howbeit, if he would procure me lodging in the town, I should take it kindly. Whereupon, sending his servants round about the town, he found at last, in the house of one of his tenants a chamber, to which, when he had conducted me, and together gotten some little accommodation for myself and horses, I desired him to depart to his lodgings, he being then in a place which his enemies, the King's soldiers, had possessed; all which was not so silently carried, but that the said nobleman was accused afterwards at the French court, upon suspicion of holding correspondence with me, whereof it was my fortune to clear him.

Coming next day to Cognac, the Maréchal de Saint-Gerant, my noble friend, privately met me, and said I was not in a place of surety there, as having offended Monsieur de Luynes, who was the King's favourite, desiring me withal to advise what I had to do : I told him I was in a place of surety wheresoever I had my sword by my side, and that I intended to demand audience of the King ; which also being obtained, I found not so cold a reception as I thought to meet with, insomuch that I parted with his Majesty, to all outward appearance, in very good terms.

From hence returning to Paris shortly after, I found myself welcome to all those ministers of state there, and noblemen, who either envied the greatness or loved not the insolencies of Monsieur de Luynes ; by whom also I was told, that the said Luynes had intended to send a brother of his into England with an embassy, the effect whereof should be chiefly to complain against me, and to obtain that I should be repealed ; and that he intended to relate the passages betwixt us at Saint-Jean-d'Angély, in a much different manner from that I reported, and that he would charge me with giving the first offence. After thanks for this advertisement, I told them my relation of the business betwixt us, in the manner I delivered, was true, and that I would justify it with my sword ; at which they being nothing scandalised, wished me good fortune.

The ambassador into England following shortly

after, with a huge train, in a sumptuous manner, and an accusation framed against me, I was sent for home, of which I was glad, my payment being so ill, that I was run far into debt with my merchants, who had assisted me now with three or four thousand pounds more than I was able at the present to discharge. Coming thus to court, the Duke of Buckingham, who was then my noble friend, informed me at large of the objections represented by the French ambassador; to which when I had made my defence in the manner above related, I added, that I was ready to make good all that I had said with my sword; and shortly after I did, in the presence of his Majesty and the Duke of Buckingham, humbly desire leave to send a trumpet to Monsieur de Luynes, to offer him the combat upon terms that passed betwixt us; which was not permitted, otherwise than that they would take my offer into consideration.

Howsoever, notice being publicly taken of this my desire, much occasion of speech was given, every man that heard thereof much favouring me; but the Duke of Luynes' death following shortly after, the business betwixt us was ended, and I commanded to return to my former charge in France. I did not yet presently go, as finding much difficulty to obtain the moneys due to me from the exchequer, and therewith, as also by my own revenues, to satisfy my creditors in France. The Earl of Carlisle[1] this while being

---

[1] James Hay, Earl of Carlisle, Knight of the Garter, Master of the Wardrobe, and Ambassador in Germany and France.

employed Extraordinary Ambassador to France, brought home a confirmation of the passages betwixt Monsieur de Luynes and myself, Monsieur de Arnauld, who stood behind the hangings, as above related, having verified all I said, insomuch that the King my master was well satisfied of my truth.

Having by this time cleared all my debts, when demanding new instructions from the King my master, the Earl of Carlisle brought me this message: " That his Majesty had that experience of my abilities and fidelity, that he would give me no instructions, but leave all things to my discretion, as knowing I would proceed with that circumspection, as I should be better able to discern, upon emergent occasions what was fit to be done, than that I should need to attend directions from hence, which, besides that they would be slow, might perchance be not so proper, or correspondent to the conjuncture of the great affairs then in agitation, both in France and Germany, and other parts of Christendom ; and that these things therefore must be left to my vigilance, prudence, and fidelity : " whereupon I told his lordship, that I took this as a singular expression of the trust his Majesty reposed in me ; howbeit, that I desired his lordship to pardon me, if I said I had herein only received a greater power or latitude to err ; and that I durst not trust my judgment so far as that I would presume to answer for all events, in such factious and turbulent times, and therefore again did humbly desire new instructions, which I promised punctually to follow. The Earl of Carlisle returning hereupon to the King, brought me yet no other answer back than that I formerly mentioned, and that his Majesty did so much confide in me, that he would limit me with no other instructions, but refer all to my discretion; promising together, that if matters proceeded not as well as might be wished, he would attribute the default to any thing rather than to my not performing my duty.

Finding his Majesty thus resolved, I humbly took leave of him and my friends at court, and went to Monsieur Savage; when demanding of him new letters of credit, his answer was, he could not furnish me as he had before, there being no limited sum expressed there, but that I should have as much as I needed; to which, though I answered that I had paid all, yet, as Monsieur Savage replied, that I had not paid it at the time agreed on, he said he could furnish me with a letter only for three thousand pounds, and nevertheless, that he was confident I should have more if I required it, which I found true; for I took up afterwards upon my credit there as much more, as made in the whole five or six thousand pounds.

Coming thus to Paris, I found myself welcomed by all the principal persons, nobody that I found there being either offended with the passages betwixt me and Monsieur de Luynes, or that were sorry for his death, in which number the Queen's Majesty seemed the most eminent person, as one who long since had hated him; whereupon also I cannot but remember this passage, that in an audience I had one day from the Queen, I demanded of her how far she would have assisted me with her good offices against Luynes? She replied, that what cause soever she might have to hate him, either by reason or by force, they would have made her to be of his side; to which I answered in Spanish, " *No hay feurza por las Reinas;* "—There is no force for Queens; at which she smiled.

And now I began to proceed in all public affairs according to the liberty with which my master was pleased to honour me, confining myself to no rules but those of my own discretion. My negociations in the mean while proving so successful, that, during the remainder of my stay there, his Majesty received much satisfaction concerning my carriage, as finding I had preserved his honour and interest in all great affairs then emergent in France, Germany, and other parts of Christendom; which work being of great concernment, I found the easier, that his Majesty's ambassadors and agents every where gave me perfect intelligence of all that happened within their precincts; insomuch that from Sir Henry Wotton, his Majesty's ambassador at Venice, who was a learned and witty gentleman, I received all the news of Italy; as also from Sir Isaac Wake, who did more particularly acquaint me with the business of Savoy, Valentina,[1] and Switzerland; from Sir Francis Nethersole, his Majesty's agent in Germany, and more particularly with the united princes there, on the behalf of his son-in-law, the Palatine or King of Bohemia, I received all the news of Germany; from Sir Dudley Carlton,

---

[1] The Vatelline; the valley stretching from the Lake of Como to the Tyrolese mountains.

his Majesty's ambassador in the Low-Countries, I received intelligence concerning all the affairs of that state; and from Mr. William Trumball, his Majesty's agent at Brussels, all the affairs on that side; and lastly, from Sir Walter Aston, his Majesty's ambassador in Spain, and after him from the Earl of Bristol and Lord Cottington, I had intelligence from the Spanish court; out of all whose relations being compared together, I found matter enough to direct my judgment in all public proceedings; besides, in Paris I had the chief intelligence which came to either Monsieur de Langherac, the Low Country ambassador, or Monsieur Postek, agent for the united princes in Germany, and Signior Contarini, ambassador for Venice, and Signior Guiscardi, my particular friend, agent for Mantua, and Monsieur Gueretin, agent for the Palatine or King of Bohemia, and Monsieur Villers, for the Swiss, and Monsieur Ainorant, agent for Geneva; by whose means, upon the resultance of the several advertisements given me, I found what I had to do.

The wars in Germany were now hot, when several French gentlemen came to me for recommendations to the Queen of Bohemia, whose service they desired to advance, which also I performed as effectually as I could; howbeit, as after the battle of Prague, the Imperial side seemed wholly to prevail, these gentlemen had not the satisfaction expected. About this time the Duke de Crouy, employed from Brussels to the French court, coming to see me, said, by way of rhodomontade, as though he would not speak of our isles, yet he saw all the rest of the world must bow under the Spaniard; to which I answered, "God be thanked they are not yet come to that pass, or when they were, they have this yet to comfort them, that at worst they should be but the same which you are now;" which speech of mine being afterwards, I know not how, divulged, was much applauded by the French, as believing I intended that other countries should be but under the same severe government to which the Duke of Crouy and those within the Spanish dominions were subject.

It happened one day that the agent from Brussels, and ambassador from the Low Countries, came to see me, immediately one after the other, to whom I said familiarly, that I thought that the inhabitants of the parts of the seventeen provinces, which were under the Spaniards, might be compared to horses in a stable, which as they were finely curried, dressed, and fed, so they were well ridden also, spurred, and galled; and that I thought the Low Country men were like to horses at grass, which, though they wanted so good keeping as the other had, yet might leap, kick, and fling, as much as they would; which freedom of mine displeased neither; or if the Low Country ambassador did think I had spoken a little too sharply, I pleased him afterwards, when, continuing my discourse, I told him that the states of the United Provinces had within a narrow room shut up so much warlike provision both by sea and land, and together demonstrated such courage upon all occasions, that it seemed they had more need of enemies than of friends, which compliment I found did please him.

About this time, the French being jealous that the King my master would match the Prince his son with the King of Spain's sister, and together relinquish his alliance with France, myself, who did endeavour nothing more than to hold all good intelligence betwixt the two crowns, had enough to do. The Count de Gondomar passing now from Spain into England, came to see me at Paris, about ten of the clock in the morning, when, after some compliments, he told me that he was to go towards England the next morning, and that he desired my coach to accompany him out of town ; I told him, after a free and merry manner, he should not have my coach, and that if he demanded it, it was not because he needed coaches, the Pope's nuntio, the Emperor's ambassador, the Duke of Bavaria's agent, and others, having coaches enough to furnish him, but because he would put a jealousy betwixt me and the French, as if I inclined more to the Spanish side than to theirs. Gondomar then looking merrily upon me, said, "I will dine with you yet;" I told him, by his good favour, he should not dine with me at that time, and that when I would entertain the ambassador of so great a King as his, it should not be upon my ordinary, but that I would make him a feast worthy of so great a person ; howbeit, that he might see after what manner I lived, I desired some of my gentlemen to bring his gentlemen into the kitchen, where, after my usual manner, were three spits full of meat, divers pots of boiled meat, and an oven with store of pies in it, and a dresser board covered with all manner of good fowl, and some tarts, pans with tarts in them, after the French manner; after which, being conducted to another room, they were shewn a dozen or sixteen dishes of sweetmeats, all which was but the ordinary allowance for my table. The Spaniards returning now to Gondomar, told him what good cheer they found, notwithstanding which, I told Gondomar again that I desired to be excused if I thought this dinner unworthy of him, and that when occasion were, I should entertain him after a much better manner. Gondomar hereupon coming near me, said he esteemed me much, and that he meant only to put a trick upon me, which he found I had discovered, and that he thought that an Englishman had not known how to avoid handsomely a trick put upon him under show of civility; and that I ever should find him my friend, and would do me all the good offices he could in England, which also he really performed, as the Duke of Lennox and the Earl of Pembroke confirmed to me; Gondomar saying to them, that I was a man fit for employment, and that he thought Englishmen, though otherwise able persons, knew not how to make a denial handsomely, which yet I had done.

This Gondomar being an able person, and dexterous in his negotiations, had so prevailed with King James, that his Majesty resolved to pursue his treaty with Spain, and for that purpose to send his son Prince Charles in person to conclude the match; when, after some debate whether he should go in a public or private manner, it was at last resolved, that he, attended with the Marquis of Buckingham, and Sir

Francis Cottington, his secretary, and Endymion Porter, and Mr. Grimes, gentleman of the horse to the Marquis, should pass in a disguised and private manner through France to Madrid ; these five passing, though not without some difficulty, from Dover to Boulogne, where taking post horses, they came to Paris, and lodged at an inn in Rue St. Jacques, where it was advised amongst them whether they should send for me to attend them. After some dispute, it was concluded in the negative, since, as one there objected, if I came alone in the quality of a private person, I must go on foot through the streets, and because I was a person generally known, might be followed by some one or other, who would discover whither my private visit tended, besides, that those in the inn must needs take notice of my coming in that manner; on the other side, if I came publicly with my usual train, the gentlemen with me must needs take notice of the Prince and Marquis of Buckingham, and consequently might divulge it, which was thought not to stand with the Prince's safety, who endeavoured to keep his journey as secret as possible. Howbeit, the Prince spent the day following his arrival in seeing the French court and city of Paris, without that any body did know his person, but a maid that had sold linen heretofore in London, who seeing him pass by, said, certainly this is the Prince of Wales, but withal suffered him to hold his way, and presumed not to follow him. The next day after, they took post horses, and held their ways towards Bayonne, a city frontier to Spain.

The first notice that came to me was by one Andrews, a Scotchman, who, coming late the night preceding their departure, demanded whether I had seen the Prince? When I demanding what prince? for, said I, the Prince of Condé is yet in Italy; he told me, "the Prince of Wales," which yet I could not believe easily, until with many oaths he affirmed the Prince was in France, and that he had charge to follow his Highness, desiring me in the mean while, on the part of the King my master, to serve his passage the best I could. This made me rise very early the next morning, and go to Monsieur Puisieux, Principal Secretary of State, to demand present audience; Puisieux hereupon entreated me to stay an hour, since he was in bed, and had some earnest business to dispatch for the King his master as soon as he was ready. I returned answer, that I could not stay a minute, and that I desired I might come to his bed-side; this made Puisieux rise and put on his gown only, and so came to the chamber where I attended him. His first words to me were, "I know your business as well as you; your Prince is departed this morning post to Spain:" adding further, that I could demand nothing for the security of his passage, but it should be presently granted, concluding with these very words; "*Vous serez servi au point nommé,*" or, "You shall be served in any particular you can name." I told him that his free offer had prevented the request I intended to make, and that because he was so principal a minister of state, I doubted not but what he had so nobly promised, he would see punctually performed ; as for the security of his passage, that I did not see what I could demand more, than that he would suffer him quietly to hold his way, without sending after, or interrupting him. He replied, that the Prince should not be interrupted, though yet he could do no less than send to know what success the Prince had in his journey. I was no sooner returned out of his chamber, but I dispatched a letter by post to the Prince, to desire him to make all the haste he could out of France, and not to treat with any of the religion in the way, since his being at Paris was known, and that though the French secretary had promised he should not be interrupted, yet that they would send after his Highness, and when he gave any occasion of suspicion, might perchance detain him. The Prince after some examination at Bayonne (which the governor thereof did afterwards particularly relate to me, confessing that he did not know who the Prince was), held his way on to Madrid, where he and all his company safely arrived. Many of the nobility, and others of the English court, being now desirous to see the Prince, did pass through France to Spain, taking my house still in their way, by whom I acquainted his Highness in Spain, how much it grieved me that I had not seen his Highness when he was in Paris ; which occasioned his Highness afterwards to write a letter to me, wholly with his own hand, and subscribe his name *your friend Charles*, in which he did abundantly satisfy all the unkindness I might conceive on this occasion.

I shall not enter into a narration of the passages

occurring in the Spanish court, upon his Highness's arrival thither, though they were well known to me for the most part, by the information the French Queen was pleased to give me, who, among other things, told me that her sister did wish well unto the Prince. I had from her also intelligence of certain messages sent from Spain to the Pope, and the Pope's messages to them; whereof, by her permission, I did afterwards inform his Highness. Many judgments were now made concerning the events which this treaty of marriage was likely to have; the Duke of Savoy said that the Prince's journey thither was, "*Un tiro di quelli cavallieri antichi che andavano cosi per il mondo a diffare li incanti;*" that "it was a trick of those ancient knight errants, who went up and down the world after that manner to undo enchantments." For as that Duke did believe that the Spaniard did intend finally to bestow her on the imperial house, he conceived that he did only entertain the treaty with England, because he might avert the King my master from treating in any other place, and particularly in France; howbeit, by the intelligence I received in Paris, which I am confident was very good, I am assured the Spaniard meant really at that time, though how the match was broken, I list not here to relate, it being a more perplexed and secret business than I am willing to insert into the narration of my life.

New propositions being now made, and other counsels thereupon given, the Prince taking his leave of the Spanish court, came to St. Andrew's in Spain, where shipping himself with his train, arrived safely at Portsmouth, about the beginning of October 1623; the news whereof being shortly brought into France, the Duke of Guise came to me, and said he found the Spaniards were not so able men as he thought, since they had neither married the Prince in their country, nor done anything to break his match elsewhere; I answered, that the Prince was more dexterous than that any secret practice of theirs could be put upon him; and as for violence, I thought the Spaniards durst not offer it.

The war against those of the religion continuing in France, Père Séguerend, confessor to the King, made a sermon before his Majesty upon the text, " That we should forgive our enemies," upon which argument having said many good things, he at last distinguished forgiveness, and said, we were indeed to forgive our enemies, but not the enemies of God, such as were heretics, and particularly those of the religion; and that his Majesty, as the most Christian King, ought to extirpate them wheresoever they could be found. This particular being related to me, I thought fit to go to the Queen-mother without further ceremony, for she gave me leave to come to her chamber whensoever I would, without demanding audience, and to tell her, that though I did not usually intermeddle with matters handled within their pulpits, yet because Père Séguerend, who had the charge of the King's conscience, had spoken so violently against those of the religion, that his doctrine was not limited only to France, but might extend itself in its consequences beyond the seas, even to the dominions of the King my master; I could not but think it very unreasonable, and the rather, that as her Majesty well knew that a treaty of marriage betwixt our Prince and the Princess her daughter, was now begun, for which reason I could do no less than humbly desire that such doctrines as these henceforth might be silenced, by some discreet admonition she might please to give to Père Séguerend, or others that might speak to this purpose. The Queen, though she seemed very willingly to hear me, yet handled the business so, that Père Séguerend was together informed who had made this complaint against him, whereupon also he was so distempered, that by one Monsieur Gaellac a Provençal, his own countryman, he sent me this message; that he knew well who had accused him to her Majesty, and that he was sensible thereof; that he wished me to be assured, that wheresoever I was in the world, he would hinder my fortune. The answer I returned by Monsieur Gaellac was, "That nothing in all France but a friar or a woman durst have sent me such a message."

Shortly after this, coming again to the Queen-mother, I told her that what I said concerning Père Séguerend, was spoken with a good intention, and that my words were now discovered to him in that manner, that he sent me a very affronting message, adding, after a merry fashion, these words, that I thought Séguerend so malicious, that his malice was beyond the malice of women; the Queen, being a little startled hereat, said, "*A moi femme, et parler*

ainsi?" "To me a woman, and say so?" I replied
gently, "*Je parle a votre Majesté comme reine, et non
pas comme femme;*" "I speak to your Majesty as a
Queen, and not as a woman," and so took my leave of
her. What Père Séguerend did afterwards, in way of
performing his threat, I know not; but sure I am,
that had I been ambitious of worldly greatness, I
might have often remembered his words; though, as
I ever loved my book, and a private life, more than
any busy preferments, I did frustrate and render vain
his greatest power to hurt me.

My book, *De Veritate prout distinguitur à Revela-
tione verisimili, possibili, et à falso,* having been
begun by me in England, and formed there in all its
principal parts, was about this time finished; all the
spare hours which I could get from my visits and
negotiations being employed to perfect this work,
which was no sooner done, but that I communicated
it to Hugo Grotius, that great scholar, who, having
escaped his prison in the Low Countries, came into
France, and was much welcomed by me and Monsieur
Tilenus[1] also, one of the greatest scholars of his time,
who, after they had perused it, and given it more
commendations than is fit for me to repeat, exhorted
me earnestly to print and publish it; howbeit, as the

---

[1] In Lord Herbert's posthumous volume of poems, a verse is addressed *To Tilenus when I had that fatal Defluxion of my Arm.* A
famous theological writer who wrote about Antichrist, and Ani-
madversions on the Synod of Dort. He was born at Goldberg in 1565
was professor of theology at Sedan, and died at Paris in 1633. He
was invited to England by James.

frame of my whole book was so different from any thing which had been written heretofore, I found I must either renounce the authority of all that had written formerly concerning the method of finding out truth, and consequently insist upon my own way, or hazard myself to a general censure, concerning the whole argument of my book; I must confess it did not a little animate me, that the two great persons above mentioned did so highly value it, yet, as I knew it would meet with much opposition, I did consider whether it was not better for me a while to suppress it. Being thus doubtful in my chamber, one fair day in the summer, my casement being opened towards the south, the sun shining clear, and no wind stirring, I took my book, *De Veritate*, in my hand, and kneeling on my knees, devoutly said these words:

"*O Thou eternal God, Author of the light which now shines upon me, and Giver of all inward illuminations, I do beseech Thee, of Thy infinite goodness, to pardon a greater request than a sinner ought to make; I am not satisfied enough whether I shall publish this book* De Veritate; *if it be for Thy glory, I beseech Thee give me some sign from heaven; if not, I shall suppress it.*"

I had no sooner spoken these words, but a loud though yet gentle noise came from the heavens (for it was like nothing on earth), which did so comfort and cheer me, that I took my petition as granted, and that I had the sign I demanded, whereupon also I resolved to print my book. This, how strange soever it may seem, I protest before the Eternal God is true, neither am I in any way superstitiously deceived herein, since I did not only clearly hear the noise, but in the serenest sky that ever I saw, being without all cloud, did to my thinking see the place from whence it came.

And now I sent my book to be printed in Paris, at my own cost and charges, without suffering it to be divulged to others than to such as I thought might be worthy readers of it; though afterwards reprinting it in England, I not only dispersed it among the prime scholars of Europe, but was sent to not only from the nearest but furthest parts of Christendom, to desire the sight of my book, for which they promised anything I should desire by way of return; but hereof more amply in its place.

The treaty of a match with France continuing still, it was thought fit for the concluding thereof, that the Earl of Carlisle and the Earl of Holland should be sent Extraordinary Ambassadors to France.

APPENDIX.

THE LADY MAGDALEN HERBERT.

THE following beautiful passage relating to Lord Herbert's mother, and casting additional light upon a period of his youth with which he himself deals summarily, occurs in Isaac Walton's *Life of George Herbert :*—

"In this time of her widowhood, she being desirous to give Edward, her eldest son, such advantages of learning and other education as might suit his birth and fortune, and thereby make him the more fit for the service of his country, did, at his being of a fit age, remove from Montgomery Castle with him and some of her younger sons to Oxford ; and having entered Edward into Queen's College, and provided him a fit tutor, she commended him to his care ; yet she continued there with him, and still kept him in a moderate awe of herself, and so much under her own eye as to see and converse with him daily ; but she managed this power over him without any such rigid sourness as might make her company a torment to her child, but with such a sweetness and compliance with the recreations and pleasures of youth, as did incline him willingly to spend much of his time in the company of his dear and careful mother, which was to her great content, for she would often say, "That as our bodies take a nourishment suitable to the meat on which we feed, so our souls do as insensibly take in vice by the example or conversation with wicked company." And would therefore as often say, "That ignorance of vice was the best preservation of virtue ; and that the very knowledge of wickedness was as tinder to inflame and kindle sin, and to keep it burning." For these reasons she endeared him to her own company, and continued with him in Oxford four years, in which time her great and harmless wit, her cheerful gravity, and her obliging behaviour, gained her an acquaintance and friendship with most of any eminent worth or learning that were at that time in or near that university ; and particularly with Mr. John Donne, who then came accidently to that place in this time of her being there. It was that John Donne who was after Dr. Donne, and Dean of St. Paul's, London ; and he, at his leaving Oxford, writ and left there in verse a character of the beauties of her body and mind. Of the first he says—

> "No spring nor summer beauty has such grace
> As I have seen in an autumnal face."

Of the latter he says :

> "In all her words, to every hearer fit,
> You may at revels or at councils sit."

The rest of her character may be read in his printed poems, in that elegy which bears the name of the

"Autumnal Beauty." For both he and she were then past the meridian of man's life.

This amity, begun at this time and place, was not an amity that polluted their souls, but an amity made up of a chain of suitable inclinations and virtues—an amity like that of St. Chrysostom's to his dear and virtuous Olympias, whom, in his letter, he calls his saint ; or an amity, indeed, more like that of St. Hierom to his Paula, whose affection to her was such that he turned poet in his old age, and then made her epitaph : " wishing all his body were turned into tongues, that he might declare her just praises to posterity." And this amity betwixt her and Mr. Donne was begun in a happy time for him, he being then near to the fortieth year of his age, which was some years before he entered into sacred orders—a time when his necessities needed a daily supply for the support of his wife, seven children, and a family ; and in this time she proved one of his most bountiful benefactors, and he as grateful an acknowledger of it. You may take one testimony for what I have said of those two worthy persons from this following letter and sonnet :—

"MADAM,—

"Your favours to me are everywhere ; I use them, and have them. I enjoy them at London, and leave them there ; and yet find them at Micham. Such riddles as these become things unexpressible, and such is your goodness. I was almost sorry to find your servant here this day, because I was loth to have any witness of my not coming home last night, and indeed of my coming this morning ; but my not coming was excusable, because earnest business detained me ; and my coming this day is by the example of your St. Mary Magdalen, who rose early upon Sunday to seek that which she loved most ; and so did I. And, from her and myself, I return such thanks as are due to one whom we owe all the good opinion that they whom we need most have of us. By this messenger, and on this good day, I commit the enclosed holy hymns and sonnets (which for the matter, not the workmanship, have yet escaped the fire) to your judgment, and to your protection too, if you think them worthy of it ; and I have appointed this enclosed sonnet to usher them to your happy hand.

"Your unworthiest servant,

"Unless your accepting him to be so have mended him,

"Jo. DONNE.

"MICHAM, *July* 11, 1607."

TO THE LADY MAGDALEN HERBERT, OF ST. MARY MAGDALEN.

"Her of your name, whose fair inheritance
   Bethina was, and jointure Magdalo,
An active faith so highly did advance,
   That she once knew more than the Church did
      know,—
The resurrection ; so much good there is
   Delivered of her, that some fathers be
Loth to believe one woman could do this,
   But think these Magdalens were two or three.
Increase their number, lady, and their fame :
   To their devotion add your innocence ;

Take so much th' example as of the name ;
   The latter half ; and in some recompense
That they did harbour Christ Himself a guest,
Harbour these hymns to His dear name addrest.

"J. D."

These hymns are now lost to us ; but doubtless they were such as they two now sing in heaven.[1]

There might be more demonstrations of the friendship and the many sacred endearments betwixt these two excellent persons (for I have many of their letters in my hand), and much more might be said of her great prudence and piety ; but my design was not to write hers, but the life of her son, and therefore I shall only tell my readers that about that very day twenty years that this letter was dated, and sent her, I saw and heard this Mr. John Donne (who was then Dean of St. Paul's) weep, and preach her funeral sermon in the parish church of Chelsey, near London, where she now rests in her quiet grave." . . . . . .

The following is an extract of Donne's commemorative sermon, mentioned above by Walton. It was delivered on 1st July 1627, at Chelsea Church, where, on the 8th June

---

[1] Dr. Grosart thinks that these hymns were not lost, but that they are to be found in his "Fuller Worthies Library" edition of *The Complete Poems of John Donne, D. D.*

preceding, Lord Herbert's mother was buried. She was the daughter of Sir Francis Newport ; her second husband, Sir John Danvers, to whom she was married in 1608, being many years younger than herself. Donne comments on this below :—

"From that worthy family from which she had her original extraction and birth, she sucked that love of hospitality (hospitality which hath celebrated that family for many generations successively) which dwelt in her to her end. But in that ground, her father's family, she grew not many years. Transplanted young from thence by marriage into another family of honour, as a flower that doubles and multiplies by transplantation, she multiplied into ten children,—Job's number and Job's distribution (as she would often remember), seven sons and three daughters. And in this ground she grew not many more years than were necessary for the providing of so many plants. And being then left to choose her own ground in her widowhood, having at home established and increased the estate with a fair and noble addition, proposing to herself, as her principal care, the education of her children ; to advance that she came with them and dwelt with them in the university, and recompensed them the loss of a father in giving them two mothers—her own personal care and the advantage of that place, where she contracted a friendship with divers reverend persons of eminency and estimation there, which continued to their ends. And as this was her greatest business, so she made this state a large period, for in this state of widowhood she continued twelve years. And then returning to a second marriage, that second marriage turns us to the consideration of another personal circumstance, that is, the natural endowments of her person, which were such as that her personal and natural endowments had their part in drawing and fixing the affections of such a person, as by his birth and youth, and interest in great favours at court, and legal proximity to great possessions in the world, might justly have promised him acceptance in what family soever, or upon what person soever, he had directed and placed his affections. He placed them here, neither diverted thence nor repented since. For as the well tuning of an instrument makes higher and lower strings of one sound, so the inequality of their years was thus reduced to an evenness that she had a cheerfulness agreeable to his youth, and he had a sober staidness conformable to her more advanced years. So that I would not consider her at so much more than forty, nor him at so much less than thirty, at that time ; but as their persons were made one, and their fortunes made one by marriage, so I would put their years into one number, and finding a sixty between them, think them thirty apiece ; for as twins of one hour they lived. . . . . God gave her such a comeliness as, though she were not proud of it, yet she was so content with it as not to go about to mend it by any art. And for her attire (which is another personal circumstance), it was never sumptuous, never sordid, but always agreeable to her quality and agreeable to her company ; such as she might, and such as others such as she was did wear." . . .

"She gave not at some great days or at some solemn goings abroad, but as God's true almoners, the sun and moon, that pass on in a continual doing of good, as she received her daily bread from God, so daily she distributed and imparted it to others.   In which office though she never turned her face from those who, in a strict inquisition, might be called idle and vagrant beggars, yet she ever looked first upon them who laboured, whose labours could not overcome the difficulties nor bring in the necessities of this life, and to the sweat of their brows she contributed even her wine and her oil, and anything that was, and anything that might be, if it were not prepared for her own table.   And as her house was a court, with conversation of the best, and an almshouse in feeding the poor, so was it also an hospital in ministering relief to the sick.   And truly, the love of doing good in this kind, of ministering to the sick, was the honey that spread over all her bread ; the air the perfume that breathed over all her house. . . . As the rule of all her civil actions was religion, so the rule of her religion was the Scripture ; and her rule for her particular understanding of the Scripture was the Church. . . . . In the doctrine and discipline of that Church in which God sealed her to himself in baptism she brought up her children, she assisted her family, she dedicated her soul to God in her life, and surrendered it to him in her death ; and in that form of common prayer which is ordained by that Church, and to which she had accustomed herself with her family twice every day, she joined that company which was about her death-bed in answering to every part thereof which the congregation is directed to answer to, with a clear understanding, with a constant memory, with a distinct voice, not two hours before she died. According to this promise, that is, the will of God manifested in the Scriptures, she expected this that she hath received, God's physic and God's music—a christianly death."

LORD HERBERT TO JAMES I.

The following letter written during his second embassy to James I., will give an idea of Herbert as an official correspondent when Ambassador to France.

"My most gracious Soveraigne,—

Now that I thanke God for it, his Highenes, accordinge to my continuall prayers, hath made a safe and happy returne unto your Sacred Majestie's presence, I think myselfe bounde, by way of complete obedience to those commandements I received from your Sacred Majestie, both by Mr. Secretarie Calvert and my brother Henry, to give your Sacred Majestie an account of that sense which the generall sort of people doth entertaine here, concerninge the whole frame and contexte of his Highnes voyage. It is agreed on all parts that his Highnes must have received much contentment, in seeinge two great kingdomes, and consequently in enjoyinge that satisfaction which princes but rarely, and not without great perill obtain. His Highnes discretion, diligence, and princely behavior every where, likewise is much praysed. Lastly, since his Highnes journey hath fallen out so well, that his Highnes is come back without any prejudice to his person or dignitie : they say the successe hath sufficiently commended the Counceil. This is the most common censure (even of the bigot party, as I am informed) which I approve in all, but in the last pointe in the delivery whereof I finde somethinge to dislike, and therfore tell them, that thinges are not to be judged alone by the successe, and that when they would not looke so highe as God's providence, without which no place is secure, they might finde even in reason of state, so much, as might sufficiently warrante his Highnes person, and libertie to returne.

I will come from the ordinarie voice, to the selecter judgment of the Ministers of State, and more intelligent people in this kingdome, who though they nothinge vary from the above-recited opinion, yet as more profoundly lookinge into the state of this longe-treated-of allyance betwixt your Sacred Majestie and Spaine in the persons of his Highnes and the Infanta, they comprehende their sentence thereof (as I am informed) in three propositions.

First, that the protestation, which the Kinge of Spaine made to his Highnes upon his departure, whereby he promised to chase away, and dis-favor all those who should oppose this marriage, doth extende no further, than to the sayd kinges servants, or at furthest, not beyonde the temporall princes his neighbours, so that the Pope, being not included herin, it is thought his consent must bee yet obtained, and consequently that the business is in little more forwardnes than when it first beganne.

Secondly, That the Pope will never yeeld his consent, unless your Sacred Majestie grante some notable privileges and advantage to the Roman Catholique relligion in your Sacred Majestie's kingedomes.

Thirdly, That the sayd Kinge of Spaine would never insiste upon obtaininge those privileges, but that hee more desires to forme a party in your Sacred Majestie's kingedomes, which he may keep always obsequious to his will, then to maintain a friendly correspondence betwixt your Sacred Majestie and himselfe. I must not, in the last place, omitte to acquaint your Sacred Majestie very particularly with the sense which was expressed by the bons Francois, and body of those of the Religion, who hartily wishe that the same greatnes which the King of Spaine doth so affecte over all the worlde, and still maintaines even in this country, which is to bee Protector of the Jesuited and bigot partie, your Sacred Majestie would embrace in beeing Defender of our Faithe. The direct answer to which though I evade, and therfore reply little more, then that this counceil was much fitter when the Union in Germany did subsiste than at this tyme ; yet do I think myselfe obliged to represente the affection they beare unto your Sacred Majestie. This is as much as is come to my notice concerninge that pointe your Sacred Majestie gave mee in charge, which therfore I have plainly layd open before your Sacred Majestie's eyes, as understandinge well, that princes never receive greater wronge, then when the ministers they putte in truste do palliate and disguise those thinges which it concernes them to knowe. For the avoydinge wherof, let me take the boldnes to assure your Sacred Majestie that those of this King's counceil here will use all means they can, both to the King of Spaine, and to the Pope (in whom they pretend to have very particular interest) not only to interrupte but yf it be possible, to breake off your Sacred Majestie's allyance with Spaine. For which purpose the Count de Tillieres hath stricte commande to give eether all punctuall advise, that accordingly they may proceede. It rests that I most humbly beseech your Sacred Majestie to take my free relation of these particulars in good part, since I am of no faction, nor have any passion or interest, but faithfully to performe that service and dutie which I owe to your Sacred Majestie, for whose most perfect health and happiness I pray, with the devotion of

Your Sacred Majestie's

Most obedient, most loyall, and most affectionate

subject and servant,

HERBERT."

From Merlou Castle, the 31st *of October,* 1623. *Stil. No.*

A PRAYER OF HERBERT'S.

A copy of the following carefully-framed prayer was found in Herbert's handwriting. It is of interest as an index not only of his devoutness, but of the character of his theological belief :—

"O God ! Thou, by whose power and wisdome all things at first were made, and by whose providence and goodness they are continued and preserved, still behold, from thy everlasting dwellinge above, me thy creature and inhabitant of this lower world, who from this valley of change and corruption, lifting up heart and eyes to Thee, his eternal God and Creator, does here acknowledge and confess these manifold blessings, these vast gifts bestowed on me ; as namely, that before I yet was, when I could neyther know nor consent to be great and good, Thy eternall providence had ordained me this being, by which I was brought into this world, a living, free, and reasonable creature, not senseless or bruitish, but capable of seeinge and understandinge thy wondrous works herein; and not only so, but of usinge and enjoyinge them, in that plentifull measure wherein they have been hitherto afforded me. O Lord, with all humbleness I confess, that were there no other pledge of thy favour than this alone, it were more than any of thy creatures in this life can possibly deserve.

But thy mercies go farther yet. Thou hast not only made me see, know, and partake thy works, but hast suffered me to love Thee for the blessings shewed us in them. I say, Thou hast admitted fraile dust and ashes to so high a dignity as to love Thee, the infinite and eternall Beauty. And not only disdainest it not, but acceptest, yea, and rewardest the same: and whence can this come, but from thy everlasting goodness, which, had it not vouchsafed to love me first, I could not have had the power (than which man has no greater) of loving Thee againe. Yet here thy mercies stay not. Thou hast not only given mee to know and love Thee, but hast written in my heart a desire even to imitate and bee like Thee (as farre as in this fraile flesh I may), and not only so, but many ways inabled me to the performance of it. And from hence, Lord, with how much comfort do I learne the high estate I received in my creation, as beinge formed in thine owne similitude and likenesse. But, O Lord, thy mercies (for they are infinite) are not bounded even here. Thou hast, then, not only given mee the means of knowinge, lovinge, and imitatinge Thee in this life; but hast given mee the ambition of knowinge, lovinge, and imitatinge

Thee after this life ; and for that purpose hast begunne in mee a desire of happinesse, yea of eternal bliss, and from thence proceeded to give mee hope ; and not only so, but also a faith which does promisse and assure mee, that since this desire can come from none but Thee, nothing Thou doest can be in vain.   What shall I say, then, but desire Thee, O Lord, to fulfill it in thy good tyme, to mee thy unworthy creature, who in this flesh can come no nearer Thee than the desireing that mortality which both keeps mee from thy abode, and makes me most unlike Thee here. Amen."

HERBERT'S IDEA FOR HIS MONUMENT.

He had, says Lloyd, "designed a fair monument of his own invention, to be set up for him in the church of Montgomery, according to the model following : Upon the ground a hath-piece of fourteen-foot square, on the middest of which is placed a Doric column, with its right of pedestal basis, and capitols of fifteen foot in height ; on the capitol of the colum is mounted an urn with a heart flamboul, supported by two angels.   The foot of this column is attended with four angels, placed on pedestals at each corner of the said hath-pace ; two having torches reverst, extinguishing the motto of mortality, the other two holding up palms, the emblems of victory."

His *Epitaph for Himself:*—

"READER,

"The monument which thou beholdest here
    Presents Edward, Lord Herbert, to thy sight :
A man, who was so free from either hope or fear
    To have or lose this ordinary light,
That when to elements his body turned were,
    He knew that as those elements would fight,
So his immortal soul should find above
With his Creator, peace, joy, truth, and love !"

———

Herbert died at his house in Queen Street, London, and was, however, buried at St. Giles's-in-the-Fields, the inscription over his grave being :—

Hic inhumatur corpus Edvardi Herbert equitis Balnei, baronis de Cherbury et Castle-Island, auctoris libri, cui titulus est, "De Veritate." Reddor ut herbæ ; vicesimo die Augusti anno Domini 1648.

———

Printed by WALTER SCOTT, *Felling, Newcastle-on-Tyne.*

OUR

AMERICAN

COUSINS:

BEING

PERSONAL IMPRESSIONS OF

THE PEOPLE AND INSTITUTIONS

OF THE UNITED STATES.

BY W. E. ADAMS.

The author brings to his work acute penetration, a keen observation, a graphic picturesque style of presenting his impressions, and a quiet humour that finds expression in quoting amusing scraps from newspaper stories and sayings that aptly illustrate the case in point.—*New York Herald.*

That Mr. Adams is a person with a power for observing closely, describing impartially, and arriving at conclusions sustained by his process of argument, cannot be doubted by those who read his interesting work.—*New York Evening Telegram.*

We can heartily recommend Mr. Adams's book to those Englishmen who want to know something about America.—*Saturday Review,* 13th October 1883.

. . . We can say emphatically and truthfully of Mr. Adams's book that it is by far the best work of its kind we have yet seen. —*Knowledge.*

. . . Altogether, it is a sober, sensible book, by a level-headed observer of men and things.—*Pall Mall Gazette,* 12th November 1883.

People who want to know what Americans are like, and how they live, cannot do better than consult Mr. Adams's work, in which they will not find a single tedious page.—*Scotsman,* 13th September.

London : WALTER SCOTT, 24 Warwick Lane, Paternoster Row.